Hungry Hurler:
The Homecoming

The Chip Hilton Sports Series

For more information on
Coach Clair Bee and **Chip Hilton**
please visit us at
www.chiphilton.com

Chip Hilton Sports Series

#23

Hungry Hurler: The Homecoming

Coach Clair Bee

Foreword by Dr. Rogers McAvoy
Updated by Randall and Cynthia Bee Farley

BROADMAN
&HOLMAN
PUBLISHERS

Nashville, Tennessee

0-8054-2125-4

Published by Broadman & Holman Publishers,
Nashville, Tennessee

Subject Heading: BASEBALL—FICTION / YOUTH
Library of Congress Card Catalog Number:
2001049930

Library of Congress Cataloging-in-Publication Data
Bee, Clair, 1900–83
  Hungry hurler : the homecoming / Clair Bee ; updated
by Randall and Cynthia Bee Farley ; foreword by
Dr. Rogers McAvoy
    p.   cm. — (Chip Hilton sports series ; #23)
  Summary: Home for the summer, college athlete Chip
Hilton hopes to occupy the restless and destructive young
people of the town by involving them in a sports program,
with an emphasis on baseball.
  ISBN 0-8054-2125-4 (pb)
  [1. Baseball—Fiction. 2. Juvenile delinquency—Fiction.]
I. Farley, Cynthia Bee, 1952– . II. Farley, Randall K., 1952– .
III. Title.

PZ7.B38196 Hu   2002
[Fic]—dc21   2001049930

1 2 3 4 5 6 7 8 9 10 06 05 04 03 02

TO

MAJOR TED DOBIAS

The heart of a marine
and the team spirit
of a football player

COACH CLAIR BEE, 1966

TO

KAREN,
with love

CINDY AND RANDY,
LUBBOCK, TEXAS 2002

Contents

HUNGRY HURLER

Foreword

NOTE: Dr. Rogers McAvoy's foreword concentrates on Dad's life and his growing up in Grafton, West Virginia. Dad incorporated a great deal of Grafton in his fashioning of Valley Falls. Because this book is a return to Valley Falls, we again welcome Dr. McAvoy's foreword to *Hungry Hurler: The Homecoming.*

Randall and Cynthia Bee Farley

CLAIR BEE grew up in the small town of Grafton, West Virginia. His ancestral history reaches back through several generations of ministers who helped establish the Seventh Day Baptist Church in the area. From these two sources, the small town and religious family background, Clair Bee acquired a set of values that sustained him through his struggles with loss and adversity.

Clair lost his mother when he was a small boy. His father remarried and had a second family, which Clair didn't quite fit into. He often spent his days roaming the hillsides above Grafton or alone reading Big Little Books or mat sports stories.

In time, in the St. Augustine gym on those same hillsides and at the YMCA on Main Street, he found an expression of himself in sports and athletics. The team and teammates became his family, coaches his father-substitute, and the game of basketball his life-long passion. Clair found in this expression of himself through sports an identity that would ultimately define and justify his life. The values of family and friends that meant so much to him had a place in sports as well as life.

More importantly, what Clair Bee was able to do in writing his Chip Hilton Sports series was to embed his cherished values within a sports setting. His message was that the common values of society and religion could be learned within the game of basketball and other sports. His hero, Chip Hilton, and Chip's friends embodied the values of family, respect, friendship, sportsmanship, loyalty, and courage to do the right thing under trying circumstances. What boy would not want to be like Chip Hilton?

Yet Clair Bee was not naive. He also knew the sad consequences of not following these accepted values. His stories contrasted these more ideal traits of Chip Hilton and his friends with youth whose behavior and beliefs varied from those of the ideal. The differences were made clear in a way that is meaningful and understandable.

Clair Bee's accomplishments as a basketball coach will always remain in the record books of basketball. His name will always be honored in all of basketball's Halls of Fame. But his true legacy will remain his Chip Hilton stories.

It is appropriate, therefore, that these books should be reissued to make them accessible to the present and

FOREWORD

future generations of youth. Each generation needs its heroes to look to for answers to its struggles. The Chip Hilton Sports series will provide for that need today as it has for generations of the past.

Dr. Rogers McAvoy
Professor Emeritus, West Virginia University

CHAPTER 1

An Ugly Encounter

HOMEWARD BOUND! The examination period was drawing to a close, and State University students were removing posters from their dorm room walls, boxing books, stereos, and computers, and excitedly packing their suitcases. The first students to leave were already stowing their gear in their cars or waiting in line at every counter at University Airport. Downtown, students jammed the University Amtrak station. Most were dressed casually in anticipation of their summer holidays. All lugged suitcases and backpacks filled with clothes and dorm treasures and gifts for family and friends back home.

The chatter and excitement at the train station rose to a crescendo, but many students paused to glance in admiration at the five male athletes gathered together near Track 7. The five were waiting for the train that would carry Chip Hilton to Valley Falls. These five athletes, campus heroes, were conference champs and members of State University's star-studded baseball team—key players who had fought hard but lost out the previous Saturday in the final game for the NCAA National Tournament.

Biggie Cohen was the biggest athlete in the group. Biggie stood six-four and weighed 240 pounds. Next to him stood Chip Hilton, State University's star pitcher. He stood four inches over six feet also but weighed in at 185 pounds. Chip's short, unruly blond hair topped off a pleasant face with friendly gray eyes. He had wide, sloping shoulders and big hands, the marks of an athlete. The other three students were all around six feet in height and solidly built. All five were hometown friends and had played sports together for Coach Henry Rockwell at Valley Falls High School before coming to State three years earlier.

As the five friends talked quietly among themselves, Soapy Smith, Chip's battery mate, stared intently at Chip. Soapy's bright-red hair set off a sunburned face dusted with freckles. Today, as he closely searched Chip's face, Soapy's eyes were a dimmer shade of their usual bright-blue color, looking like the ocean on an overcast day. "You feel all right?" he asked Chip.

"Of course I do, Soapy. Stop worrying and quit looking over your shoulder."

"How can I? It was my fault," Soapy grimaced.

"No," Biggie growled. "*I* lost the game when I fumbled the ball."

Chip knew his pals were trying to shoulder the blame for the loss of the championship game, trying to ease the bitterness that had been chewing at their hearts ever since Western defeated them for the national championship. "Cut it out," he said shortly. "Pitchers lose the games."

Speed Morris shook his head, and his large hand squeezed Chip's shoulder. "I wish we were going with you, man."

"No big deal," Red chimed in. "We'll all be home Saturday. Don't worry, Chip. Soapy and I will make sure we bring the rest of your stuff with us in the car."

"How come Doc wanted you home tonight?" Soapy asked.

"You've got me, Soapy. All I know is that Doc sent me an E-mail saying to be in Valley Falls tonight. Here, read this. I printed his message out." Chip unzipped his backpack and pulled out a folded piece of white paper.

Soapy unfolded the message and studied it with Speed, Biggie, and Red looking over his shoulder.

CAPTAIN CHIP HILTON
www.chiphilton.com

Hi Chip,
Your mother said your exams are completed. I would appreciate your coming
home to Valley Falls on Thursday. I have a
possible important summer job for you, and
there's a meeting I need you to attend on
Friday morning. There's a problem—some
personal trouble—and I need your help.
Sincerely,
Dr. R. Jones

"Sounds kind of mysterious. What do you think he means by 'personal trouble'?" Soapy asked, returning the E-mail.

"I don't know, Soapy."

"It doesn't really sound like Doc," Speed offered, frowning. "And it's hard to imagine *him* sending an E-mail, isn't it?" The observation was met with grins.

"Hey, here she comes!" Red called. The Amtrak train braked and glided past them before grinding to a stop.

Chip grabbed his duffel bags and hoisted his backpack to his shoulder. Soapy quickly tucked the latest issue of *Sports Illustrated* into the side pocket of the backpack. He patted the bag. "For the train, Chipper!"

Chip waved good-bye to his four friends and climbed aboard. At the top of the stairway, he turned and lifted his right hand in a farewell salute. "See you Saturday, guys!"

The smell of strong coffee and the humid air of the train assaulted Chip's senses as soon as he entered the passenger car. He quickly found his seat and stowed his duffels. Grinning, he remembered to pull the magazine out of his backpack before placing it on the railing above his head. After the train pulled out of University Station, Chip watched the city fade into countryside and then glanced through the magazine. But he couldn't concentrate.

His thoughts sped back to the previous Saturday's championship game and the pitching problem that had plagued him ever since he had beaned a Southwestern batter during a conference game. Gradually he forced the unpleasant occurrence out of his thoughts and focused instead on Valley Falls and Doc Jones and the summer job that was so important.

His thoughts shifted to his mother, and his chest tightened. His father, William "Chip" Hilton Sr., had lost his life in an accident at the Valley Falls Pottery many years ago. Over time, his mom had worked her way up into management at the phone company in Valley Falls. Somehow she had managed to hold onto their house and built a home for the two of them. She had gotten him through high school. And now, although he was helping with his college expenses by working, his mom was still carrying most of the burden. Someday, Chip had promised himself, he would make it up to her.

It was a restful trip, but he was glad when it was over. The train slowed down for the Valley Falls railroad yards, and Chip lifted his bags down from the rack and glanced at his watch. In a few minutes he would learn what it was all about. He would know more about the job Doc Jones had lined up, and, above all, he would know what his old friend meant by "personal trouble."

Chip looked out the window. It was a beautiful June afternoon and white, fleecy clouds hovered almost motionless in the sky. The bright sun, slowly dipping in the west, cast a warm glow on the landscape. Familiar sights met his eyes now: the long rows of railroad cars standing on the yard tracks and, beyond these, the gentle river where he had learned to swim. The wide, placid stream meandered through the center of town, and little ripples from the current caught and glistened in the sunlight.

"Valley Falls!" the trainman called from the front of the car. "This way out."

Chip was the first person down the steps to the platform. He knew his mother would just be getting off work, but he looked for her just the same. He spotted Doc Jones moving toward him. The large man still walked at a fast pace, but Chip noticed he favored his right leg a little and so his gait was slightly lopsided. His old friend's face was wreathed in smiles, and Chip breathed a sigh of relief. Doc appeared to be in good health.

John Schroeder, Chip's former employer, and Petey Jackson, the new manager and soon-to-be owner of the Sugar Bowl, followed Doc. They met in the center of the platform, and Chip dropped his bags and shook hands with each of his old friends. Petey picked up the duffel bags then and led the way through the crowd. Doc Jones and John Schroeder, who were both talking to Chip at the same time, each grabbed one of his arms, and the three of them followed Petey.

Up ahead on the landing, in front of the main waiting room, several young men in their late teens or early twenties were lounging in front of the doorway. Chip glanced up just in time to see them suddenly close ranks in front of Petey Jackson. Standing shoulder to shoulder, they left no room for Petey to pass through.

"Look who's here," one of them said, affecting an air of surprise. "If it isn't the Sugar Bowl boy! And a big shot sports figure."

"Are you crazy?" another chimed in. "He's no big shot. Petey's just the manager of the town ball club. You know—the cellar dwellers."

Petey moved to the right and then to the left, but each time one of them blocked his path. "Come on, guys," he pleaded, "we're in a hurry."

"We're in a hurry," a mocking voice echoed.

Petey tried once more to walk around the group. This time, a taller, heavier man waved his companions aside and shoved Petey roughly back. "You aren't going anywhere until we're ready."

Chip, seeing this, was torn by a sudden, violent burst of anger. Petey was an old friend, and he wasn't going to stand by and watch him be humiliated. Struggling to fight back the anger that engulfed him, he started forward. But Doc Jones beat him to it. He sprang quickly up the steps and moved purposefully toward the leader. "What are you trying to do?" he demanded sharply. "Move out of the way."

"Sure, Doc," the husky fellow said condescendingly. "Don't get all worked up. We just wanted to have a little fun with Petey. You know how it is—"

"No, I *don't* know how it is," Doc Jones retorted angrily. "Now move out of the way."

"Sure, Doc," the fellow said mockingly. "Sure."

The arrogant posture and taunting tone filled Chip with an urge to knock the grin off the speaker's face. He moved forward, half hoping the leader would remain in Doc's path. But the bulky fellow winked at his companions and moved slowly to one side.

Chip scanned their faces, noting the cocky, amused expressions. Then he looked squarely at the leader, sizing him up. The face was familiar, but Chip couldn't place him. He was about nineteen, maybe twenty, six-two, but at least fifteen pounds heavier than Chip. The fellow smiled mockingly before turning away. Chip reluctantly followed Doc into the station. "I won't forget *you*," he said softly to himself.

Doc's car was parked across the street in front of the bus station and right in the middle of the space reserved for taxis. Doc was a special person in Valley Falls, and Chip was usually intrigued by the physician's eccentricities. Now, however, he was upset. The ugly events of the past few minutes had left him shocked and angry. There had to be some connection between Doc's E-mail and the ugly encounter.

Doc got into the car without a word, and Petey Jackson placed Chip's bags in the backseat. Chip turned to say good-bye to his other two friends as John Schroeder grasped his hand. "See you tomorrow morning, Chip."

"Drop in tomorrow at the Sugar Bowl," Petey added soberly. "Doc said something might happen."

Chip was still upset, and Petey's reference to a meeting occupied his thoughts for only a second. He got in the front seat, and the physician drove slowly and carefully up Main Street. Doc's face was still flushed with anger; the older man was deep in thought. His old friend's preoccupation gave Chip a chance to review the incident at the station. Why had those fellows acted that way toward Petey?

When he and Petey had worked together at the Sugar Bowl, Petey had been a fighter. No one pushed Petey around in those days. There was only one way to find out, Chip concluded.

"What was wrong with those guys, Doc?" he suddenly asked.

"I wish I knew," Jones said grimly.

"The big guy, the leader . . . was that Jerry Blaine?"

Doc nodded. "That was Jerry Blaine. You know the family."

Chip knew the Blaines, and he remembered Jerry. They were a big family, all boys and men it seemed. The Blaine name was synonymous with trouble. "Yes," Chip said, "I know them. But what made them act that way?"

"There's nothing else to do in this town," Jones said bitterly.

"Jerry and those fellows at the station—do they have anything to do with the trouble you mentioned in your E-mail?"

"I'd rather not talk about it just now," Doc said, glancing sideways at Chip. "Anyway, you'll find out soon enough. There's a town board meeting at nine o'clock tomorrow morning in Mayor Brooks's office, and I'd like to take you along. All right?"

"Sure, Doc."

Changing the subject, Doc commented, "I bet you're looking forward to getting home and seeing your mother."

"Yes! I can't wait! It's been a long time."

Doc drove up the hill and turned onto Beech Street. The tree-lined road flooded Chip with memories of his boyhood. Doc pulled into the driveway at 131 Beech

Street and honked the horn. The large oak tree beside the white colonial house was alive with fresh buds, and Mary Hilton's pink and white impatiens lined both sides of the walk.

Just then Mary Hilton walked onto the porch and then hurried down the steps to greet her son, her blond hair streaked golden by the early evening sunlight. The blast from the horn had startled Hoops, the gray cat. He was eyeing the scene and stretching to wakefulness on his favorite wicker chair on the front porch.

"This *is* a wonderful surprise," Mary Hilton said happily, hugging Chip. "I just got home myself. When Doc told me you would be home tonight, I could scarcely believe it. I didn't expect you until Saturday with the rest of the boys."

"Thanks for the ride, Doc," Chip said, pulling his bags out of the backseat. "It was nice of you to meet me."

Mary Hilton nodded in agreement. "That goes for me, too, Doc."

The old physician grunted and shifted the car into gear. "I'll pick you up tomorrow morning at 8:30," he said. Then, as the car backed slowly out of the driveway and into the street, he added, "You're going to run head-on into the biggest challenge of your life."

CHAPTER 2

The Greatest Athlete

MARY HILTON was bewildered. She looked questioningly at Chip for a moment. "Now what in the world did he mean by that?" she managed.

"I don't know, Mom."

"Well," she said, shrugging her shoulders, "let's get into the house. I bet you're hungry. Why don't you take your things upstairs and shower while I get dinner started? You can make us a salad when you come down."

Chip showered and changed into a pair of old shorts and a State sweatshirt and then hustled down the stairs to join his mother in the kitchen. She had already set the table. Chip fed Hoops and then gathered together a head of lettuce and other salad fixings.

"I wonder what Doc was talking about?" his mother began again.

"I don't know. He said something about attending a town board meeting first thing in the morning. I promised to go, but I'd rather be out looking for a job."

"You'll find something," Mrs. Hilton said confidently. She hesitated a moment and then continued. "I read about the game in the paper. Do you want to talk about it?"

"I'd rather not."

"I know you did your best," his mother said gently. "When you're ready to talk about it, you know I'll be ready to listen."

After dinner Chip and his mom worked together to clear the table, rinse the dishes, and load them into the dishwasher. Later, they went into the family room, talked about school for a time, and then did some reading until it was time to go to bed. Chip was tired. It felt great being back in his own room and in his own bed, but he just couldn't get to sleep. His thoughts skipped from one thing to another: getting a summer job, Doc's trouble, and his own pitching problem. Chip tossed and turned from side to side, trying to fall asleep. Hoops finally gave up. He meowed his complaint and left to seek a peaceful sleep somewhere else. After what seemed like hours of tossing and turning, Chip finally fell into a troubled sleep.

Doc Jones stopped by for him precisely at 8:30 the next morning. Doc drove slowly downtown, deep in thought. Respecting the physician's mood, Chip remained quiet and tried to puzzle out the reason for *his* presence at the board meeting. He was sure of one thing at this point. The E-mail, the incident at the station, and the board meeting were all tied in with Doc's plea for help.

Jones parked in a space directly across the street from the Valley Falls Town Hall. "C'mon," he said gruffly, dropping some coins in the meter. "Let's get upstairs to the mayor's office. It should be interesting."

Once inside the building, the physician and Chip mounted the cold marble steps of the massive entryway lined with portraits of venerable citizens and the founders of the town. On the second floor, Doc Jones motioned for Chip to follow. Walking resolutely down the hall, the physician knocked on the door to the mayor's private office. A heavy voice called, "Come in," and then Doc opened the door, stepping aside so Chip could pass through.

Chip stopped just inside the room, glancing quickly about. The heavy-shouldered man sitting behind the desk near the windows was Mayor Brooks. Other members of the board, most of whom Chip knew, were sitting on a variety of straight-backed chairs situated around the room but all facing the mayor's desk.

"Mayor Brooks, this is Chip Hilton," Doc said, gesturing toward the young athlete.

The mayor got to his feet and extended a broad, heavy hand. "Glad to meet you, Hilton. Welcome to our meeting."

"You know J. P. Ohlsen and John Schroeder, of course," Jones continued, his eyes twinkling at the mention of his longtime friends. Chip shook their hands and smiled warmly. Along with Petey and Doc, John Schroeder had greeted him at the train station. Chip had worked after school and weekends at the Sugar Bowl for the kindly man during his high school years.

J. P. Ohlsen had been a fixture in the Hilton family's life for as long as Chip could remember. Until the accident that had suddenly taken his life, Chip's father had worked as chief chemist for Ohlsen at the Valley Falls Pottery. But times had changed, and Ohlsen had recently sold the pottery to an international group that had upgraded the technology. J. P. still served as a consultant and traveled to various ceramics conferences as an esteemed speaker, however.

"This is Henry Hawkins," Jones said, jerking his head toward the next member of the board. "Henry is president of the Valley Bank. And," he continued, "I'm sure you remember Anthea Narbond, a real estate developer."

With the exception of Henry Hawkins, each board member smiled and shook Chip's hand as Doc Jones introduced him. The fourth board member, who was much younger than any of the other board members, stood up and moved quickly toward him. "I'm Dick Troll," he said, grasping Chip's hand. "It's a pleasure to meet you."

"District attorney," Doc added. He waved a hand toward a chair beside the mayor's desk. "Sit down over there, Chip."

Ill at ease, Chip sat down on the straight-backed chair and glanced around the office. Every person in the room was an important personality in Valley Falls's civic affairs. He felt uncomfortable and out of place.

The mayor cleared his throat and shifted his feet restlessly on the floor. "Chip," he said, "I don't know how much Doc told you about this meeting, but it might help if you just sat back and listened." Resting his elbows on the desk and supporting his large, shaggy head with the palms of his hands, he turned toward Jones and continued, "All right, Doc. Tell us how we're going to clean up the mess we have on our hands."

Jones glanced uncertainly at the empty chair beside Hawkins and then walked across the room and leaned against the windowsill. "All right," he said, "I'll start with a question. What's our biggest problem?"

"Teenagers," Troll said quickly. "Kids with nothing to do and too much time on their hands and too many temptations around."

"What about the town toughs?" Hawkins demanded. "What about the Blaines and their north-side packs? *They're* not kids. *That's* where the trouble starts. They're always starting fights with the high school kids."

"That's not true," Jones said curtly, glancing at Hawkins. "The high school boys are as much to blame as the others. They speed their cars around town at all hours of the night and race up and down the north-side streets yelling and whooping. They're just looking for trouble, and they're beginning to find it."

"If you're referring to my—" Hawkins began angrily.

Mayor Brooks rapped the desk with his knuckles. "Just a moment now," he said, the color rising to his forehead. "Let's give Doc a chance."

Doc Jones eyed Hawkins speculatively for a long moment. "If Valley Falls could provide jobs for our young people, most of the trouble would be eliminated."

"You can blame Mike Hogan for that," Hawkins said angrily. "Here we are with a five-year project on our doorstep and not a single Valley Falls resident can get a job."

"We ourselves are chiefly responsible for that situation," Jones said. "When Mike Hogan and his construction crew arrived here in Valley Falls with their families and trucks and house trailers, we gave them the cold shoulder and brushed them off. They got the message and kept right on going. They rambled on up the river to the project site, set up their tents and trailers, and built their own town. Had we been halfway decent to Mike Hogan and his tunnel crew, there would have been plenty of jobs."

Chip's nervousness disappeared as he became absorbed in the discussion. The reason for his presence had begun to come into focus. It *was* the kids. And also, he reflected soberly, older kids and even some of the more solid people in town.

"*Adults* are usually at fault when youngsters get into trouble," Doc continued. "Anyway, we've got to find a way to dilute the tension that's building up in this town, or we're going to run into some real trouble."

"Going to!" Hawkins replied sarcastically.

Mayor Brooks cleared his throat. "Well," he said, "what's the answer? Where do we go from here?"

No one spoke. During the long, heavy silence that followed, Chip's thoughts were racing. He now had the solution to the question, the something that had disturbed him ever since the incident at the station. The attitude of the teenagers had incensed him, but evidently that was only a small part of the problem in Valley Falls. It went deeper, much deeper than a teenage problem. It was just as much an adult predicament.

Brooks turned to Chip. "There you have it, Hilton. We've got to find something for the kids and young men of this town to do. We need to find a way to heal the breach between them and keep them from fighting and getting into trouble. Doc thought you might be able to make some suggestions."

Every person in the room turned toward him. They were waiting quietly but expectantly. Chip tried desperately to think of something to say, but he drew a blank. It was the same sort of mental paralysis he had experienced in the Southwestern game when one of his fastballs had beaned the SW captain. What was there to do with teenagers and older fellows in the summertime?

During his younger days, the summer months had meant going away to camp for his friends whose parents could afford it. But to Soapy, Biggie, Speed, Red, and himself, it had meant freedom from school, playing ball on a neighborhood team, and going fishing and swimming in the river near the fairgrounds. As a youth, he was always doing something with the guys. Why wouldn't a summer sports program like that still keep kids, even teenagers, busy and happy?

"About all I can think of," he said tentatively, "is some sort of a sports program."

"Could we open the high school facilities during the summer?" Schroeder mused aloud.

"Why not?" Troll asked. "The only problem is finding supervision and money for salaries."

"Not salaries," Brooks said, forcing a laugh. "A salary. One!"

"How about Coach Curtis?" Anthea Narbond asked.

"He's not popular with the kids," Jones said shortly. "Anyway, he has to run his camp."

"Curtis does all right with his camp baseball team," Brooks said. "He wins the Valley championship every summer."

"Naturally," Jones agreed. "That's the reason, or one of the big reasons, the summer league is a flop. All the other teams use local players or hometown college players. Curtis brings 'em in from all over the country. He won't hire a counselor unless he's a college star."

"It seems to me we're getting a bit ahead of ourselves," Schroeder observed. "We ought to decide first whether we want to go along with the idea."

"I'm for it," Brooks said decisively.

"Well, I'm not!" Hawkins said shortly. "We're moving too fast. We ought to have a few more meetings to discuss the situation."

"That's what we *always* do," Troll said hotly. "We meet and meet and meet. Let's *do* something for a change."

"Amen," Schroeder said softly.

"Mr. Mayor," Troll said, "I move we hire someone to supervise a summer sports program for boys and young men at the high school."

Brooks looked at Schroeder. "Got that, John?"

Schroeder nodded, and Brooks glanced at each board member in turn. "Any debate?" he asked.

"No debate," Hawkins said bitterly. "What's the use? But I want to go on record as being opposed to this whole idea. If you turn the high school over to the kids, it will be in shambles before the summer is over."

"Very well, Henry," Brooks said softly. He looked at Schroeder and nodded gravely. "Be sure to include Henry's objection in the minutes, John."

The mayor called for a show of hands. Everyone except Hawkins voted in favor of the motion.

"The ayes have it," Brooks said calmly. "What's the next step?"

"Finding someone for the job," Troll said.

"I know just the person," Doc said quickly.

"Who?"

"The greatest athlete to come out of Valley Falls in the past twenty years!"

CHAPTER 3

A Boy in a Man's Job

"CHIP HILTON!" Anthea Narbond said quickly, nodding her head toward Chip. "Of course! There's no doubt about it."

Chip's heart jumped, and he felt the blood rush to his face. *They surely can't be considering me for the job*, he thought wildly.

Doc Jones nodded. "Right. Every kid in town knows Chip. Or knows about him. He's a natural for the job."

"Chip would be great," Narbond said enthusiastically. "Kids look up to successful athletes—I know my son and his friends would follow Chip Hilton like . . . well, like the Pied Piper!"

Hawkins grunted. "That," he said sarcastically, "I've got to see!"

Chip started to interrupt, but Doc checked him with an impatient wave of his hand. "Well?" he said, looking steadily at Brooks.

"What if Chip isn't interested?" Brooks asked.

"He's interested," Chip blurted out.

Chip hardly knew he'd said it. Now he *was* in for it. Why hadn't he kept his mouth shut? Doc must have had something like this in mind all along. Hadn't he said something about a challenge? Sure he had! *Doc had planned the whole thing,* Chip mused.

Narbond cleared her throat. "I suggest you offer Hilton the job, Mayor," she said firmly.

"I go along with that," Troll added.

"Me too," John Schroeder agreed.

"Wait a minute!" Hawkins said irritably, rising to his feet. "I know Hilton is a great athlete, and I know he's popular. But he's only a youngster. He's too young to handle adult problems."

Hawkins paused, glanced at Jones, and continued pointedly. "I also realize that some of the members of this board have been subjected to a tremendous amount of pressure, even brainwashed. But there *is* a limit. I strongly resent the creation of a project to provide anyone with a job. However, if you must do something to impress the voters, I suggest that you at least refrain from putting a boy in a man's job."

Chip wanted to melt, to sink through the carpeted floor and out of sight. His ears were burning and his heart was thumping furiously. He wanted to tell Mr. Hawkins that he hadn't even dreamed of applying for the job; he hadn't even known a job would exist. But the words wouldn't come. Suddenly he felt a surge of anger, and several phrases formed in his mind. He started to his feet, but before he could speak, Jones interrupted.

"Nonsense!" the physician said roughly. "Growing-ups can handle grown-up problems. The trouble is, people like you won't give them a chance."

"Hilton is the man for the job," Troll said firmly. Doc, John Schroeder, and J. P. Ohlsen nodded.

"That's good enough for me," Brooks said. He rose from behind his desk and grasped Chip's hand. "The job is yours, young man. Do you have anything to say?"

Chip was completely overwhelmed. It was a tremendous undertaking, and as the magnitude of the responsibility permeated his mind, he felt a premonition of trouble. But Henry Hawkins's attitude and words had made a greater impact. He wasn't going to forget what the banker had said about putting a boy in a man's job.

"It's a wonderful opportunity," he said awkwardly. "I'll do my best."

"Good!" Brooks said with approval. "We'll start the program Monday morning at the high school. Now," he concluded, glancing around the room, "unless there is further business to come before the board, this meeting stands adjourned."

The members of the board were on their feet almost as soon as the mayor finished speaking. Suddenly, it seemed to Chip as if they were trying to escape from a responsibility. They seemed relieved because the burden had been shifted to other shoulders.

Hawkins paused at the door and snorted disdainfully. "To have a special meeting for this sort of nonsense! I can put my time to better use." He left the room, closing the door sharply behind him.

"Perhaps he should devote a little of his time to his own son," Troll murmured.

Narbond and Schroeder shook hands with Chip and followed the banker. Troll shook Chip's hand firmly. "We're behind you all the way, Chip," he said. The district attorney then nodded to Brooks and Doc Jones and left the room.

"Sit down, Chip," the mayor said, gesturing toward the chair beside his desk. "You've got yourself quite a job, a tough one. Nothing was said about your salary, but I was considering three dollars an hour over minimum wage. How does that strike you?"

"That's fine, Mr. Mayor."

"Good. We'll start the program next Monday morning, July 1. Bill Sherman, the buildings and grounds superintendent, will be at the high school to help you get started. Hustle over to the *Sentinel* office now and tell Jim Butler what happened here this morning. I want to be sure to get the story in tomorrow's paper. We need to make the parents aware of the program as quickly as we can. You remember Sherman from your own high school days, I guess."

Chip nodded. "Yes, sir, I do."

Together, Chip and Doc Jones retraced their steps down the marble stairs and out into the street. Doc, crossing the street, said he had a quick errand to run and that he would then wait for Chip in the car. Chip continued on around the corner to the *Sentinel* office. Through the glass window on the street level, Chip could see Jim Butler working at a large desk in the corner of the room. The sports editor rose swiftly to his feet when Chip opened the door to the office.

"Hello, Hilton," Butler said, grasping Chip's hand. "Welcome home! It's great to see you. The mayor just called me. Here, sit down by my desk and tell me about the program."

Chip outlined his plans as best he could. When he finished, Butler checked through a file and came up with a glossy print. "It's one of State's baseball shots," he explained. "I'm running a story about last Saturday's game in this week's paper, and it will fit in fine with the recreation program." He paused and smiled. "I don't suppose you want to make a statement about the game?"

Chip shrugged. "The better team won. That's about all."

"Well, it took the championship team to beat you. Be sure to read Saturday's paper."

Chip located a pay phone in the hall of the building and called his mom at the phone company. "Hi, Mom!" he said excitedly. "Guess what! You won't believe this. I've got a job working for Mayor Brooks. Doc was responsible. I'll tell you all about it tonight." They said good-bye, and Chip joined Doc in the car.

Doc said nothing until they had gone several blocks. "Well, young man," he said, "what do you think about your new job?"

"It's a big challenge."

Doc nodded soberly. "That it is. By the way, you haven't said anything about the game. Tell me about it."

"There's nothing much to tell, Doc. Too bad I was pitching, that's all."

Doc grunted and sliced a look at Chip. "That's a silly, ludicrous statement if I ever heard one," he said shortly.

"It's not ludicrous, Doc," Chip said quietly. "It's serious. I've pitched my last game."

CHAPTER 4

Beanball Dilemma

DOC JONES jammed his foot down on the brake pedal and pulled to a stop at the curb. "Pitched your last game?" he repeated incredulously. He peered over his glasses at Chip, his eyes wide in astonishment. "Why, you're one of the best pitchers in the country. Any pitcher can lose a ball game. You can't be serious."

"I mean it, Doc."

"Nonsense!"

"You don't understand. I froze. Completely. You remember the Southwestern player I beaned? Well, in the championship game, in the bottom of the thir- teenth inning, the Western players began to crowd the plate, and I couldn't throw a curveball or a slider to save my life. I was afraid I would hit one of them. It's difficult to explain, but I just couldn't force myself to use any kind of a tight pitch. The team didn't lose the championship. I did!"

"I never thought I'd see the day Chip Hilton would back away from a challenge," Doc said slowly, his eaglelike eyes narrowed to slits. "It's not like you to walk away from baseball just because you lost a game."

"It wasn't just a game, Doc. It was an entire season, a lifetime for some of the guys, maybe their last chance ever to be on a national championship team. You know about all the trouble between the sophomores and the veterans and the players we lost because of bad grades. Well, anyway, the players came back every time. They fought through to win the conference and the sectionals and then battled their way to the NCAA finals. I don't know how they did it."

"I do!" Doc said grimly, his black eyes snapping. "*You* know too. In fact, you said it yourself. You said it was a *fighting* ball club. Well, you fought too. How come you can't fight now?"

"I'm not afraid to fight. I'm afraid I'll hit a batter with a ball and kill him. It *has* happened."

"Of course it has. That's the reason batters wear helmets. You're not the first pitcher to have beanball trouble. What do air force pilots do when they wreck a plane? That is, if they can walk. You tell me."

"They go right back up."

"Right! So?"

"But they have only themselves to worry about. It's different when someone else, a whole team, is involved."

Doc stared straight ahead for a long, long time. When he turned back toward Chip, his voice was sharp and angry. "Now you listen to me, youngster. Baseball is a man's game. Accidents are bound to happen. Ballplayers take chances every time they face a pitcher, dive for a line drive, or slide into a base. You never threw an intentional beanball in your life. There are hundreds of pitchers who have hit batters with a ball. All pitchers face that possibility. It's part of the game."

"But why do I freeze up? If I could eliminate that, it would be easy."

"Nothing worthwhile is easy. You have to whip this beanball trouble all by yourself, on your own. Start over. Walk out on the mound every chance you get and whip your own problem. And another thing to consider is this: the only person involved *now* is yourself."

"I don't think it'll work, but I'll sure try," Chip said quietly.

"Time will tell," Doc said shortly. "Now I'll drive you home."

Chip spent the rest of the morning at home scraping and painting the front door and making minor repairs to the house. While he worked, his thoughts centered around his new job. Everything had happened so fast he had been knocked off balance. Where would he start? What had made him think a sports program would bring all the bitter factions together? It was a frightening prospect, and the more he thought about it, the more impossible it seemed.

Around two o'clock Chip was in the flowerbed pulling the dead blossoms off the azalea plants. Petey Jackson drove up and parked his car at the curb in front of the house. "Hey, Chip," the new Sugar Bowl proprietor called as he got out of the car, "how about going over to the baseball camp at Clarksville?"

Chip shook his head. "I'm tired of baseball, Petey."

"It would give you a chance to see Stu Gardner again. He's doing some clinics at the camp. Remember him? He's the guy who tried to sign you to a Yankees contract when you were in high school."

Chip smiled and nodded. "I remember."

"Come on, let's go."

"On one condition. You have to drive past Tunnel Town."

"Sure," Petey agreed. "We've got lots of time." Together they climbed into the car.

Petey drove down the hill and across the bridge to the north side; then he turned west on the river road. It ran parallel to the river and passed the old fairgrounds, which were less than a mile from Main Street.

"Too bad," Petey said, motioning toward the racetrack. "That was John Schroeder's white elephant. When you and I were kids, it was a great thing for the town, but it's been boarded up for years. Times change."

It was the opening Chip had been waiting for, a perfect chance to clear up Petey's side of the trouble with Jerry Blaine and his gang. "You've changed too," he said. "How come you let Blaine push you around at the station last Thursday?"

Petey's fingers tightened on the wheel. "Jerry was just trying to show off," he said casually, "trying to imitate his brother. You know Speck."

Chip nodded. He remembered Speck Blaine well enough. Everyone in Valley Falls knew Speck was a north-side tough who seemed to always be mixed up in a fight.

"Only one more mile," Petey continued. "You won't believe your eyes."

"Come off it, Petey. I'm not blind. I can see what's going on. Why don't you stand up to them? You used to fight back."

"Things are different now. Fighting doesn't solve problems anymore, Chip. I've changed. . . . I'm a Christian now. I try to treat people right, and I'm happier for it. Besides, next year Jackie and I are getting married. I have to think about responsibilities. I've just about finished my business degree—Mr. Schroeder helped me get into State's extension college. He and I have an agreement. Once I complete my degree, I'll take over the Sugar Bowl, paying him monthly installments until it's mine. I have to think about my future."

"What about your self-respect?"

"You don't understand," Petey said wearily. "I can't fight them all alone."

"Doc Jones is fighting."

"Yes, but he's not getting anywhere." Petey paused and shook his head. "I know what Doc has in mind, Chip. He's counting on you to interest the kids in sports, to substitute athletics for loafing and fighting. I don't happen to think it will work."

"You'll help, won't you?"

"Of course! I'll say this too. If anyone can do it, you can."

Chip dropped the matter, and a short distance later Petey took the right fork in the road that led away from the river. After a hundred yards or so they reached a point above the construction site, and Petey slowed down and parked.

"There you are," he said, waving his hand at the scene below.

Petey had been right. It was hard to believe his eyes. Directly below them, a tremendous tower was surrounded by a bewildering array of heavy construction equipment. Men and equipment were loading dozens of trucks with shattered rock drawn from deep under the river.

"The shaft goes down four hundred feet," Petey said. "The dam will take about five years to complete."

"Where's the town?"

"On up the hill."

They took one last look before Petey drove the car back onto the main road. In a few minutes they were at the top of the hill and the road leveled off. A hundred yards farther and they were in the center of a small group of buildings lining each side of the road. Behind these buildings, arranged in street formations and extending in both directions, were scores of house trailers. Farther up, away from the river, rows of neatly painted houses were visible.

"It's a regular town," Chip said.

"Sure is. Seemed to have sprung up overnight. Seen enough?"

"For the present."

Petey stepped on the gas. "Good. Clarksville, here we come."

They reached Clarksville in half an hour and parked in the lot adjoining the fenced-in baseball field. "Same old stadium you used to play in," Petey said.

They walked through the main gate and into a bedlam of baseball. There must have been a hundred players scattered over the field, and the bleachers were jammed with kids. A tall, slender man, clad in a Yankees uniform, was conducting infield practice, but when he saw Chip he stopped and waved.

"Who's that?"

"Stu Gardner, the man you were talking about," Chip explained.

Gardner turned the clinic over to an assistant and joined them. Although Chip had seen the scout in the stands at some of the State University games, it had been quite a while since Chip had actually talked to Stu Gardner. Chip would have known him anywhere. The man was tanned, fit, and alert. "Hello, Chip," he said, grasping Chip's hand. "This is a surprise. Where's your uniform?"

"Back at State, and it's going to stay there. I've had enough baseball. Oh, Mr. Gardner, this is Petey Jackson."

"Glad to meet you, Jackson," Gardner said, extending his hand. "Are you a ballplayer?"

"Not me," Petey said.

"He manages the Valley Falls community team," Chip explained.

"By the way," Gardner said, "how about meeting the men? All right?" He blasted his whistle and the players came sprinting in, demonstrating baseball's number-one quality—hustle! The scout waved toward the bleachers, and the players quickly filled the seats.

When they were settled, Gardner introduced Chip and Petey. Then the scout selected two teams and the practice game got underway. Rejoining Chip and Petey, the scout pointed out some of the better players and discussed their strengths and weaknesses. Chip and Petey left before the game ended but promised Gardner they would try to see him again before the end of the camp.

Chip preceded Petey out through the main gate and almost stumbled over a young teen who was leaning disconsolately on one of the entrance railings. The boy was clad in a makeshift baseball uniform and looked so forlorn that Chip stopped and moved back against the other railing. He waited for the boy to look up, but the youngster didn't move, which gave Chip a chance to size him up.

The slumped shoulders, bowed head, and frustrated expression on the boy's face spelled discouragement. Chip studied the face a little more closely, noting the firm chin and the thin, determined lips. He measured the wiry frame and then his glance shot toward the boy's hands. Hands make the difference in sports. The fingers on this boy's hands were long and slender. They were strong talons capable of grasping a ball with the looseness an athlete needs to generate speed. Chip judged the boy to be fourteen or fifteen years old and figured his weight at around 140 pounds.

"Hi," he said. "You see the workout?"

The boy looked up and nodded his head, a light of recognition flashing into his eyes. "Sure," he said. "I wanted to try out, but they wouldn't give me a chance."

"What position do you play?"

"I'm a pitcher."

Chip explained that the tryout guys were older, that some were college students. "You're a little young for that group," he concluded gently.

"You talk just like my brother," the boy said, his eyes flashing angrily. "He's captain of a team, but he never gives me a chance. No one does. No one *ever* watches me throw. Not even my father, and he loves baseball. Everyone calls me a kid and that's not right. I read in a Hall of Fame booklet that the legendary Bob Feller was pitching big-league ball when he was sixteen. I'm *fifteen*."

"You said it yourself; he's legendary. There aren't many Bob Fellers," Chip said gently.

"I know," the boy said, "but I'm still going to be a pitcher."

"What's your name?"

"Michael."

"All right, Michael, let's take a look. Got a ball?"

"Sure," the boy said, extending his glove hand. "I carry a ball with me all the time. Wherever I go."

Several boys had been edging up while they were talking. One of them had a catcher's glove, and Chip borrowed it. "Back up sixty feet and let's have a catch."

The boy threw a dozen pitches, putting a little more into his delivery each time until he was throwing fairly hard. He had good speed; the ball seemed to smack into Chip's glove before his delivery was completed. Chip waved his throwing hand from right to left, the signal for a curve, and the boy responded immediately with a sidearm motion that whirled the ball in toward Chip's glove hand.

"How about a change-up?" Chip called, returning the ball.

"I use my curve. I throw it slow."

The boy gathered his stretch and, seemingly, released the ball with all his might. But it was sheer deception, and Chip nodded in approval when the ball came whirling lazily toward him. It was well done. "Nice going," he called. "That's enough."

But it wasn't enough for the rest of the kids. They crowded around him, waving papers for autographs and asking all sorts of questions. When Chip finished signing the last outstretched paper and looked around for Michael, the boy had disappeared.

During the return trip to Valley Falls, Chip and Petey talked about the sports program and how much it could mean to teenagers like Michael. Then the conversation lagged, and Chip lapsed into his own thoughts.

Visiting the baseball camp had brought back all Chip's baseball bitterness. As the car sped steadily along, he relived the events that had led up to the disastrous championship game: The beanball pitch in the Southwestern game. The fears that had dogged him every time he tried to throw a slider or a curveball. His unsuccessful fight to whip the problem, and, finally, the loss of the national championship game.

Well, Soapy and Biggie and Speed and Red would be home tomorrow. He had a good job, and he was going to try to forget his big flop as a pitcher. He closed the door on the old memories of the game and his frustration. He knew one of these days he needed to face the situation, but he wasn't yet prepared to do so.

CHAPTER 5

A Big Undertaking

MARY HILTON was watering the hanging flowers on the front porch when Petey stopped the car in front of the house.

"Thanks, Petey," Chip called as he bounded up the porch steps. "I'll see you tomorrow." Arm in arm, Chip and his mom waved until the car had rounded the bend and was out of sight. Then they walked over to the porch swing.

Chip scooped up a sleepy Hoops from the wicker chair. "Lazy cat!"

Mary Hilton smiled expectantly and patted the seat. "OK. I've been waiting all day. Tell me all about the job, Chip."

"Well, first, it's a job for Valley Falls, and I'll be supervising a summer recreation program at the high school. The salary is good—three dollars over minimum wage, and I start Monday."

"Monday! That doesn't give you much time to get yourself organized."

"Mayor Brooks was in a hurry to get the program started."

"No wonder," Mrs. Hilton murmured. She paused for a moment and then, as if reaching a decision, turned on the swing to face Chip. "Valley Falls has changed, Chip. It's still basically a good town with good people, but there are some real problems and animosities. The mayor and police just can't seem to control our young people." She hesitated and shook her head worriedly.

"Some time ago," she continued, choosing her words carefully, "Doc Jones wrote an article for the *Sentinel* and really came down on the boys and young men for their bad behavior."

"Good!"

"Not so good."

"Why not?"

"Because someone retaliated by throwing rocks through the windows of his office and slashing the tires on his car."

"Oh, no!"

"It's true," his mother sighed in resignation. "That's not all that's been going on. Petey Jackson stood up for Doc and got in an argument with some of the young toughs and they—someone—threw rocks through his storeroom windows and released stench bombs in the Sugar Bowl."

"What about the police?"

"There's only Chief Burrows and Mr. King. That's all this town has ever needed before, but now the two of them just can't keep up with all the troublemakers. Every week the paper is full of reports of speeding, boys cited for juvenile court, burglaries, attempted break-ins, and fighting between the high school boys and the boys from the north side. There's also a real fear that the kids with too much time on their hands are dabbling in drugs. I wish you hadn't taken the job."

"It isn't easy to say no to Doc Jones." He thought that over for a moment and then nodded his head affirmatively. "I'm glad I did take it!" he said fiercely. "No wonder Doc is worried."

"It's a big undertaking," Mrs. Hilton acknowledged. "First thing you had better think about is getting some help. Why don't you ask Rick Reilly and Taps Browning? You know they like you. They're both home from college, and I don't think they're working. Why don't you go over and see if Taps is home?"

"Good idea."

Chip went through the house, out the kitchen door, down the back porch steps, and then hopped the fence between the Hilton and the Browning homes— just as he had a hundred times when he and Taps were students together at Valley Falls High School. Taps was a sophomore at a private engineering school, and although the two friends often E-mailed, they had not seen each other for quite some time. As soon as Chip rapped on the kitchen door, all of Taps's six feet and seven inches filled the door. "Chip! All right! Come in!"

As Chip was unfolding his plans to Taps, a tall girl dressed in running clothes bounded through the back door, her long brown hair tied up in a ponytail. Perspiration beaded on her brows and just above her lip. "Chip! You're home!" she exclaimed.

"Suzy? Wow, what happened to you?"

"I grew up. It happens. I graduated and I head off to college in the fall."

"You're still running, I see."

"Running and soccer! My two loves."

"Soccer!" Chip declared. "That's perfect! Can you sit down for a minute?"

A BIG UNDERTAKING

About thirty minutes later, Chip went home, and soon his mother called him to the table. "We're celebrating!" she declared. She had prepared his favorite meal: fruit cocktail, roast beef, mashed potatoes and gravy, Yorkshire pudding, green beans, salad, and vanilla ice cream.

As they were eating, Chip sniffed the air appreciatively at the wonderful aroma emanating from the oven.

"That's a chocolate cake," Mary Hilton grinned. "I know Soapy will be home tomorrow."

When they finished their ice cream, Chip sighed and shook his head. "Two months of this and I'll be too fat to walk."

After the kitchen was shipshape, Chip called Rick Reilly, who said he would be glad to help. Afterward, Chip jogged up to the high school and back and then spent the rest of the evening with his mom talking about school and his new job. He had not realized how tired he was until he was between the sheets at ten o'clock. In a short time he was asleep, with Hoops purring contentedly at his feet.

> The umpire crouched behind the plate, and there was the poised hitter and his long, long bat. Soapy's catcher's glove seemed to be a target as big as a satellite dish. But Chip couldn't move, couldn't lift his arms, couldn't take his stretch, couldn't fire the ball toward the plate. He was paralyzed!
>
> The crowd noise increased to a deafening pitch, and he resumed his straining and pulling, trying again and again and again to throw the ball. Then, at last, with a mighty effort, he forced himself forward and made the pitch.

That effort broke the spell, and Chip awakened to find himself sitting bolt upright in bed, his pitching arm in final forward motion.

Wet with perspiration and shaken by the dream, Chip settled back in bed. He had been playing the Western game all over again! He had frozen in the dream just as he had in the final game for the championship. He glanced at the clock and came fully awake.

It was ten o'clock in the morning, and his mother had already been gone for almost two hours. He dressed and hurried downstairs, his thoughts shooting ahead to the *Sentinel* and Jim Butler's story. The paper was on the porch and the recreation story was on the front page. Glancing at the headline, he went into the dining room and spread the paper out on the table.

His picture in a State University baseball uniform and cap was located directly over the article.

CHIP HILTON HEADS RECREATION PROGRAM
High School Sports Fields to Be Used

Mayor Brooks announced last night that the town council has authorized the creation of a summer sports recreation position and named William "Chip" Hilton, State's three-sport all-American, to supervise the program.

Interviewed yesterday at the offices of the *Sentinel,* Hilton stated that special leagues and tournaments in baseball and basketball would be important features of the program. He urged all interested persons between the ages of ten and twenty-one to enroll. The hours: 9:00 to 12:00 and 2:00 to 5:00 p.m. Monday through Friday, starting July 1.

A BIG UNDERTAKING

Directly below the recreation article was an announcement about the Valley Baseball League. Chip glanced at it casually and started to pass over the story, but when he saw Petey Jackson's name, he continued reading to the end.

VALLEY BASEBALL LEAGUE REORGANIZED

A meeting of the Valley Baseball League managers was held last Wednesday evening at the Clark Hotel in Clarksville. Petey Jackson represented Valley Falls at the meeting.

The managers were firm in their determination to make this the best season in the history of the league. It was decided to play a double-elimination series instead of a formal schedule as had been used in the past and to intersperse the schedule with exhibition games played against nonleague teams. This innovation will provide a varied diet of baseball for the fans.

The season opens next Saturday, July 6, with Camp Curtis meeting Valley Falls at the high school field. Bradford plays at Martinsburg on the same day. All Wednesday games will be limited to seven innings.

The following organizations and towns will be represented in the league: Valley Falls, Camp Curtis, Bradford, Martinsburg, Clarksville, The Colts, Brighton, and Tunnel Town. The Colts, Brighton, and Tunnel Town are new entries.

Cap Curtis, owner-director of Camp Curtis, the perennial champions of the Valley, announced that Lefty Slavin, star pitcher of the NCAA champions, Western University, had been added to his camp staff as a head counselor.

"Lefty Slavin," Chip murmured. "In Valley Falls of all places."

Directly below the league story was a brief summary of the State-Western championship game and the box score. Chip knew that by heart. Skipping over it he read the last paragraph.

> With Chip Hilton home for the summer and Lefty Slavin at Camp Curtis, Valley Falls baseball fans just might have an opportunity to see these two great stars in another pitchers' duel before the end of the summer. Stranger things have happened.

"Oh, sure!" Chip murmured. Folding the newspaper, he tossed it on the table and went into the kitchen. His mom had thoughtfully set a place for him at the counter. He microwaved some frozen pancakes and drank a large glass of milk. After eating he washed his plate and glass and went outside to mow the lawn and do some pruning.

Chip had just finished raking and bagging the grass and was putting the mower away in the garage when he heard the car horns honking. A welcome sound! Speed's Mustang, followed by Red's SUV, were just pulling into the driveway.

"Chip, my man, we're home!" Speed drawled.

"Does your mom have any of her wonderful chocolate cake?" Soapy hollered, bounding out of the passenger side of Red's SUV.

Chip laughed and nodded his head. "Of course mom has some cake. She knew you were coming home today."

By this time, the five friends were standing together on the front lawn, and Chip addressed each in turn.

"Welcome home, Speed."

"Hey, Biggie!"

"How ya doin', Red?"

"Did you miss me, Soapy?"

"Tell him the good news," Soapy said eagerly.

"Right!" Speed added. "Go ahead, Red, tell him."

"Well," Red began, "I called my dad last night, and he's got jobs for you and me and Biggie and Soapy—for all of us, except lawyer boy," he added with a nod at Speed. "Dad's construction company just got a big contract. A new housing development's going in at Brighton. He's got jobs for all of us."

Talking all at once, they filled Chip in on the details. "Everything's all set," Red said excitely.

"The best is yet to come," Speed added. "I'll be clerking in a law firm in the very same town! Can you believe it? And this year Brighton has a ball club in the Valley League. We're all going to play on the team."

"We can practice every evening," Soapy explained. "Say! What was wrong with Doc Jones?"

"I'll tell you about it later. Anyway, I can't take the job at Brighton, Red. I got a job from Mayor Brooks, working for the town."

There was a tense silence. His friends looked from one to another, shocked surprise and disbelief written on their faces. Soapy recovered first. "You mean we're not going to be together?" he said incredulously. "Chip, the job with Mr. Schwartz is what we've been hoping for all along."

"I know, Soapy. I'd like nothing better, but I can't back out now."

"What kind of a job is it?"

"Running a recreation program at the high school."

"Can't you get out of it?" Soapy persisted.

"No, I can't. I accepted the job, and I've got to stick it out."

"Playground stuff," Red snorted. "Anyone can run a playground."

"It's for Doc," Chip said quietly. "He asked me to do it and got me the job, so I've got to follow through."

"But Doc said it was trouble," Soapy added.

"I know," Chip agreed. "He also said he needed help."

CHAPTER 6

A Surprised Bully

KIDS, KIDS, KIDS! Boys and girls. All sizes, all shapes, all eager, and all excited. Some arrived in cars with their mothers, while others walked—singly, in pairs, and in small groups. Many of them carried basketballs and soccer balls and baseball gloves and bats. Here and there a boy or girl appeared with a tennis racket and a can of balls. Some were dressed in baseball uniforms and others in shorts and T-shirts. All wore sneakers.

Soapy's twin cousins, dressed in Little League baseball uniforms, were there, poignantly reminding Chip that this was the first time in a long time that he and the redhead were not working side by side. Soapy's cousins were identical twins, twelve years old, and smaller counterparts of Soapy. Both had red hair, blue eyes, freckled faces, and square shoulders.

The kids were still coming at 9:30. Chip was forced to close the gate momentarily and keep the overflow waiting until he could register those already on hand.

He had stationed Taps Browning at the basketball courts, Rick Reilly on the baseball field, and Suzy Browning on the soccer field. And, as fast as he could write down the children's names and addresses, he directed them to the areas of their chief interest. He was hoping some of the high school athletes would show up, but not one of them put in an appearance. All the boys and girls appeared to be around ten, eleven, and twelve years old.

By the time everyone was registered in the attendance book, Taps, Rick, and Suzy had their groups organized and were working on hoop, baseball, and soccer drills. There were only five or six tennis players. Chip found the one who, by popular vote, was the best and put him in charge.

Rick, Taps, and Suzy were enthusiastic and good with the kids. That night they gathered in the Hilton family room to work on the program. Just before they left, Chip asked them what the teenagers thought of the program.

"They think it's good," Rick said, "but they don't want to mix in with the little kids."

Wednesday morning, the Smith twins were at the head of the line. "Soapy called home last night from Brighton," the first one said.

"He's coming home Saturday afternoon," the second one added.

The program worked smoothly, and at five o'clock Petey and the community team players appeared. They took over the baseball field for their own practice. Chip decided to pay a visit to Doc Jones's house. Ten minutes later he turned in at the gate. He walked up the broad steps to the big porch and rang the doorbell. Doc opened the door and peered at Chip over his glasses. "It's about time," he said with a smile. "I was expecting a report. Come in."

A SURPRISED BULLY

The physician led the way into the big, high-ceilinged living room and motioned to a chair. "Care for a Coke or coffee or something?" he asked.

"Nothing except advice."

"It might cost you big money. What do you want to know?"

"How to win over the high school and north-side gangs."

Doc smiled and folded his hands across his large belly. "You don't want much, do you? Well, first, you don't win over gangs. You win their leaders. Now let me think about it a bit." He leaned back in his chair, moving his hands from his stomach to his head. After a few minutes, he continued, "Let's start with the north-siders, Chip. They aren't really bad fellows. They only act tough to cover up a sense of inferiority because there's nothing else to do. If Mike Hogan would give them jobs at the tunnel and dam project, they would have a chance to prove themselves, to earn respect. They act rebellious to prove they *are* somebody."

"They seem to be full of hate."

"Not all of them."

"How about the Blaines?"

"Well, Chip, I guess I know the Blaines about as well as anyone. Just like I did you, I brought them into this world too. Now take Jerry. He's a strong boy, but he doesn't have the mental toughness that is one of Speck's strong points. Jerry is a leader without a cause who carries a terrific inferiority complex.

"Speck isn't big like Jerry. He can't weigh more than 160 or 170. But ever since their father died, Speck has been the head of the family and, except for an occasional binge, he's done a pretty fair job. Speck could have been a great athlete if someone had taken him in hand when he was a youngster. As I said before, his greatest enemy is liquor. When he goes on one of his binges, he *really* flips. He's as dangerous as a rattlesnake, and everyone gives him a wide berth.

"Jerry is deathly afraid of Speck, yet he tries to imitate him. But Jerry doesn't have the hardness that sets Speck apart from most of the toughs around town. Speck is mean-tempered; he never backed away from a fight in his life. But, in his way, he's honest in everything he does. And, because Speck is honest, you will find that Jerry is honest."

"How could they be won over?"

Jones rubbed his chin and gazed reflectively at the ceiling. "Well," he drawled, "that would be quite a chore. Frankly, I think Speck would be your best bet, but I haven't the slightest idea how you could approach him. If you *could* sell it to him, you would have the north side locked up tight."

"How about the high school kids, Doc?"

"Well, the high school kids' big heroes are Rip Redding and Billy Jo King. You know both of them, of course. Except they've grown up a bit since you were in high school. Rip is almost another Chip Hilton, except that he's a lefty first baseman and about the size of Biggie Cohen. He's an excellent student too.

"Billy Jo weighs about 220. He has, in my opinion, the makings of the greatest African-American athlete in the history of the state. He plays football, basketball, and baseball *and* he's a top student. You might say those two are the present-day Chip Hilton and Speed Morris of Valley Falls! Anyway, those two have three or four buddies who are almost as good. If you win them over, the high school kids will follow."

"There has to be a way," Chip said fiercely, rising to his feet.

Jones got wearily out of his chair and followed Chip into the hall and out onto the porch. Then, before turning back, the physician added, "Where there's a will—"

A SURPRISED BULLY

Chip said good night and walked thoughtfully along the quiet street. "Where there's a will, there's a way," he murmured. Well, he had the will; and because Doc had said the way to success was to win leaders, he might as well get started. Doc had listed Jerry or Speck Blaine, one of them, at the top of the list. That was where he would begin. He needed to make contact.

Deep in thought, he cut down the hill to Main Street. There were only a few people in sight, but suddenly, up ahead, he saw the 7:30 crowd spilling out of the Main Street movie theater. Most of the crowd walked toward Chip, going up Main Street toward the business section, but two small groups turned in the same direction Chip was heading.

Chip noticed there were three girls and one boy in the first group. They walked along leisurely. Fifty feet or so behind them, three older fellows moved forward at a slightly faster pace.

He gave little thought to either group. However, as the first group approached the bus station, the second party closed the gap. Chip now looked at the latter group more closely and his heart leaped. One of the three was Jerry Blaine, the very person he had been thinking about! What a coincidence.

Now Blaine and the two with him quickened their steps. They were swiftly overtaking the first group. The purposefulness of their advance attracted Chip's attention, and on a sudden hunch he stepped up his own pace, drawing closer to Blaine and his two companions.

Then it happened!

Jerry must have said something insulting to the boy because the youngster whipped around and replied angrily. Before he could finish, Jerry stepped forward and grabbed the boy by the neck, roughed him up, and then threw him into the street. One of the girls tried to interfere, but Jerry's two companions pushed her roughly aside.

Chip waited to see no more. A sudden, overpowering rush of righteous anger broke loose in his entire being, and this time he made no effort to stop it. Springing forward, he grasped Jerry's arm and spun him around. Then, as he waited for Jerry to get set, Chip caught the gleam of exultation in the bully's surprised eyes.

Jerry started a swing, but Chip stepped swiftly forward, inside the blow, and drove a straight left to Jerry's face. He followed up with a second punch that carried all the weight of his shoulders. The blow caught Jerry flush on the chin. It was a beautiful one-two combination, and Jerry stumbled slowly backward, dropping to a sitting position on the sidewalk. He ended up against the wall of the building. For a brief moment, Chip looked at the glazed eyes staring uncomprehendingly up at him. Then, he turned back to the two men who had accompanied Jerry.

They were staring in disbelief at their fallen leader. Then, when Jerry failed to get to his feet, they turned and came at Chip in a solid rush. He stepped back until his shoulders touched the wall of the building and waited, his heart and brain filled with burning fury for the lot of them. Furious anger gripped every fiber of his being. How could a bunch of fellows manhandle a boy and girl just for kicks?

He knew fighting wasn't a good solution, but sometimes difficult situations couldn't be avoided. Chip's conscience was clear in that respect. To him, not interfering would have been a mistake; he knew well enough that those who are bullied need protection.

Then they were on him, clawing and punching, both trying to get at him at once, pushing one another aside in their eagerness. A hand rasped across Chip's cheek, and one of the men caught him in the eye with a glancing blow. Chip set himself again and retaliated with a straight right, flush on the bully's chin, sending the roughneck staggering backward. The other one came barreling in and tried to tackle him around the knees. But, at the last second, Chip sidestepped and drove his knee forward. The would-be tackler rolled away holding both hands to his face.

The remaining fellow hesitated uncertainly. Chip turned to look at the girl who had tried to help. She was standing near the curb holding her fists to her mouth, her eyes wide with fear. The other two girls were standing close to the building and beyond them he could see the waiting bus, the driver and the passengers looking out at the scene.

The boy who had been walking the girls home had scrambled to his feet and was moving toward Chip. Now, as the young teenager got closer, Chip recognized him. It was the pitcher, the kid from Clarksville!

"Hey!" Chip said quickly, "Michael! What are you doing here? I thought you lived in Clarksville."

The boy hesitated a second. "No," he said in a low voice, "I live in Tunnel Town."

"Good!" Chip said. "Let's get on that bus before there's more trouble."

Several spectators were emerging from the bus station, and others were peering out the windows. Across the street, in front of the Amtrak station, some men were standing on the curb. Now they began to move slowly toward the scene.

The incident had lasted only a few seconds and the lull for only a moment, but it gave Chip a chance to gain some measure of self-control. The white heat of passion slowly drained away, leaving him weak and shaken. Now he wanted only to get the boy and the girls on the bus.

The tackler, holding his hands to his face, looked at Blaine. The other one had backed off; he was waiting for Jerry to determine the course of action. All three were unsure of themselves, and Chip seized the opportunity to act. He grasped Michael's arm and joined the girls. "Let's hurry up and get on the bus," he said, urging them along.

"OK, Hilton," Jerry called, motioning his companions away. "That was just the first round. Next time it'll be different."

"I'm sorry it had to happen," Chip said. "You gave me no choice."

He walked on with the little group until they reached the steps to the bus. The driver was ready to pull out, and he closed the door as soon as Michael and the girls reached the platform. Chip waved to them and turned away. Then he realized that he hadn't learned Michael's last name. What's more, he hadn't even asked the boy to come out for the recreation program.

Blaine and his two companions had disappeared, but several bystanders were still on the scene. They were talking in low voices and covertly watching Chip. As he approached, they moved back, leaving a roomy path for him to walk through.

"You sure gave it to them, Hilton," one of them said in admiration.

"Got what they deserved, they did," another added. "Jerry Blaine bit off more than he could chew that time, he did."

Chip kept going, but he glanced at them and nodded. He was still shaken by the encounter. As he walked along, he berated himself for his lack of emotional control. He had let his personal revulsion for Jerry Blaine overcome his sense of judgment. He should have tried to stop the affair without becoming involved in a fight. At least, he told himself, he could have tried.

Now, not ten minutes after he had left Doc Jones, he had botched up the very first part of his program. Things couldn't be much worse, but, as Biggie would have said, it didn't do any good to look over your shoulder. And since Rip Redding and Billy Jo King were next, according to Doc's list of leaders, he might as well see if he could botch that meeting up, too, right now, tonight!

Perennial Champs

TEN MINUTES LATER, Chip was walking up the stone steps in front of the Redding home. The house was dark, but when he reached the terrace, he could see a lighted TV screen through a window. He knocked on the screen door, and seconds later Rip appeared in the hall. Rip snapped on the porch light and opened the door at the same time. For a moment he looked at Chip with wide-eyed surprise, then he managed a grin. "What happened to you?" he asked. "You look like you've been in a fight. Come in. I've been watching a sports show."

Chip followed Rip through the hall and into the living room. The big high school athlete turned on the light, shut off the TV, and motioned to a chair. "Sit down, Chip," he said, smiling warmly. "It looks like you're gonna have a black eye. You've got a scratch clear across your face too. What happened?"

"Nothing much. Just a little run-in with Jerry Blaine."

"Didn't he have his gang with him? I've never seen him without two or three of his roughneck pals."

"He had a couple with him," Chip said, sizing up the tall high school star. Rip stood at least four or five inches over six feet and was well put together. "You've grown since I last saw you," Chip noted. "You're almost as big as Biggie."

"Almost is right," Rip said. "I wish I could be half the ballplayer he is."

"I hear you're a pretty good first baseman."

Rip laughed self-consciously. "Not really," he said, "at least not in Biggie's class. Tell me about the fight. Did you tangle with all three of them?"

"It was just a scuffle and didn't last more than a couple of seconds," said Chip. "I came to see you because I was wondering if you and some of the other high school guys could lend a hand with the recreation program in your spare time. I guess you know about it."

Rip nodded. "Everybody knows about it, Chip."

"There's no money in it, but I'm sure you would get a kick out of helping the kids."

"I guess I could help," Rip said thoughtfully. "I work at Reed's waiting tables on weekends, but I could help during the week."

"How about Billy Jo King?"

"I'm sure Billy Jo would help if he isn't working."

"Where does he live?"

"You know Murdock's store? Over on the north side?"

"Sure."

"Billy Jo lives three doors past the store, on the same side of the street. But you'd better be careful. Jerry and his gang hang out at Murdock's. Do you want me to go with you?"

"No, thanks. I'll be all right. I'll see you Friday morning, OK?"

"I'll be there. I guess you heard that Lefty Slavin, the Western pitcher, is going to work at Camp Curtis."

Chip nodded. "Yes, I did. He's a great pitcher, Rip."

"Maybe so. Anyway, I'd sure like to see you tangle with him once more."

"Not much chance of that, I guess."

"You've tackled a tough job," Rip observed quietly. "Most of the people in town know what you're up against and what the board is trying to do. You can count on me, and I'm sure Billy Jo will feel the same way."

He hesitated before continuing and shook his head uncertainly. "About the rest of the high school guys, I'm not sure. About all a lot of them think about is cars and girls and playing it cool. Sure, they're mostly good kids, but you'll need something *big* to bring *them* around."

"I know," Chip said. "So far, I haven't been able to think of anything."

"You will," Rip said confidently. "Going to the game tomorrow? It's part of the celebration with Curtis playing the Valley League stars. Slavin's supposed to pitch part of the game."

"I'll probably go," Chip said, rising to his feet. "Thanks for your help. Meet me at my house about 8:30 Friday morning. OK?"

"OK."

Rip accompanied him to the porch and said good night. He was still standing there, leaning against one of the porch posts, when Chip turned the corner. Chip, taking a shortcut to the north side, crossed the railroad bridge and then struck across the field next to the fairgrounds. A few minutes later he neared Murdock's store. A few boys were loafing on the sidewalk and they watched him curiously as he approached. They didn't say anything as he passed, but after he had taken a few strides he heard one of the boys say, "That was Chip Hilton."

"You *sure?*"

"Yes. Of course I'm sure. His picture was in the paper."

He reached the third house and walked up on the porch of the brick two-story home and knocked. A husky elementary-aged boy, who looked him up and down, opened the door.

"Does Billy Jo King live here?" Chip asked.

The youngster nodded slowly. "You want to see him?"

"I'd like to."

"Wait right here," the boy said. He closed the door partway and backed slowly into the room. A minute or so later he was back, followed by his brother.

Billy Jo was about Speed's height, but he was wide and thick through the middle, a real heavyweight. A flash of recognition crossed his face as he approached. "Hello, Chip," he said eagerly. "Come in. You looking for me?"

"I sure am. I haven't seen you in a long time, but you haven't changed much."

A smile lit up Billy Jo's face. "Got wider," he said, patting his waist. He turned to his brother. "Now you head to bed, little brother."

Chip told Billy Jo about his visit with Rip. Then, he explained the summer program and asked for his help. Billy Jo nodded understandingly. "I know the problems, Chip. It seems like this town doesn't have plenty of anything except trouble anymore. How come you took on a job like this?"

Chip explained the challenge and his desire to help Doc Jones. "I grew up here. I still think of Valley Falls as home, Billy Jo. It was a great and healthy—well, supportive—place for me to grow up. I want it to *always* be a great place for kids to grow up. Right now, it just doesn't seem to be." Chip went on to tell Billy Jo about the difficulty he was facing with the high school teenagers and the older guys. "It's a little discouraging," he concluded.

"Especially when you run into guys like Jerry Blaine," Billy Jo said. "I heard about your run-in with him tonight. He and Turk—that's his younger brother—are bad trouble. Both of them are good baseball players, but they only want to loaf around and look for fights."

"News travels fast."

"When it concerns the Blaines," Billy Jo explained sourly. Then his voice changed. "Sure, Chip," he said, "I'll help. The only job I have is the checkout at the grocery store, and that's part time. We have a big family; and I tried to get on the crew at the tunnel, but I didn't have any luck."

"Rip is meeting me at my house Friday morning at 8:30. You know where I live?"

"Doesn't everybody in Valley Falls?" Billy Jo said, grinning. "I'll be there."

They walked out on the porch. A quick glance was enough to tell Chip that the number of guys hanging out in front of Murdock's had increased. "Well," he said, "I guess I'd better get along home."

"I'll walk along with you a ways," Billy Jo said.

The group was watching them and talking in low voices, but when they reached the store, conversation ceased. Several of the boys spoke to Billy Jo, and a few nodded in Chip's direction. After they passed, talking resumed on a louder note as if an argument was developing. At the bridge, Billy Jo said good night and promised to look him up at the game the next afternoon.

Chip's mother noticed his swollen eye and the scratch on his face as soon as he walked into the house.

"What happened?" she asked, her voice rising with alarm.

He told her about the fight, trying to pass it off as unimportant so she wouldn't worry. Shortly afterward, he went to bed.

The next morning, Chip got up early and started for the Sugar Bowl. When he reached Main Street, the big Fourth of July parade was underway. The lampposts and storefronts were festooned with red, white, and blue drapings, and the American flag decorated every building. Beautifully decorated floats, high school bands from Valley Town and Valley Falls, Scout troops in uniforms, a National Guard color guard, war veterans, the mayor, members of the town board, and local and state politicians passed by in endless procession.

Chip found Soapy, Biggie, Speed, and Red at the Sugar Bowl, talking to Petey. They had heard about the scrap and wanted to know the details. Chip put them off and turned the talk to the recreation program.

"I hear you have a full house," Biggie said.

"All little kids. What kind of a ball club have you got?"

"It's great now," Soapy answered. "Of course, it wasn't much until *we* showed up, naturally."

Biggie took a swipe at the redhead but missed. "We could use a good pitcher," he said. "How about it?"

"No can do, Biggie."

They talked for a time about the Brighton team and their jobs and then agreed to meet at the game. Biggie and Red took off in Red's SUV, and Speed drove Soapy and Chip home, letting Chip out first. After lunch, Chip walked to the high school and paused just inside the entrance to the field to look for his friends. Like all Valley League games, no admission was charged and good seats were a matter of first come, first serve. He finally located the guys. They were sitting in the bleachers behind third base; Rip and Billy Jo were directly behind them. Chip walked around the bleachers, made his way up the steps, good-naturedly elbowed the two high school stars apart, and sat down between them.

Curtis was taking final fielding practice, and Lefty Slavin was warming up beside third base. He was putting on quite a show, and the catcher helped out by making each pitch crack loudly when the ball smacked into his mitt. Fans were yelling to the star, and Slavin waved slowly in return as he lazily tossed the ball to the catcher.

"He thinks a lot of himself, doesn't he?" Billy Jo said in a low voice.

"That's about all he does think about," Soapy growled.

Coach Curtis hooked an arm, and the Curtis players ran off the field. They were confident, full of pep, and looked like a real ball club. All were college stars, but Chip knew only Lefty Slavin.

Petey Jackson walked out to home plate with a portable mike in his hand and made the introductions. He introduced the Curtis players first. Some of the names were familiar, but they meant nothing to Chip. And, as Rip had said, there wasn't a State player on the roster. Petey then introduced the all-stars. Most of them were older, and Chip recognized various names. Some of them had been stars when he was in high school. There was only one player from Brighton.

"How come you guys aren't playing?" Billy Jo asked, tapping Biggie on the shoulder and motioning toward the field.

"They're s'posed to be league veterans," Biggie explained.

"Then how come Slavin is playing?" Rip asked.

"Because Coach Curtis wouldn't let his team play without him," Soapy said. "At least that's what Petey Jackson told me."

"That's not right," Rip protested.

"Might makes right," Billy Jo said tersely. "If Coach Curtis says it's right, it's right."

When the player introductions were completed, the umpire advanced to home plate and announced the Curtis battery. The camp team ran out on the field and Lefty Slavin sauntered out to the mound. The all-stars got their first look at Lefty Slavin's pitching wares. The southpaw was in good form, and his port side slants set them down in order.

Curtis scored two runs in the bottom of the inning, and Slavin held the stars scoreless for the next three innings. Then he retired in favor of another of Coach Curtis's pitching greats. Chip had been studying each of the Curtis hitters, mentally cataloging their hitting styles and possible weaknesses. It was clear that all were good players and that they had recently finished college seasons. Camp Curtis fielded a solid-hitting ball club, and with Slavin pitching the team seemed to have everything it needed to repeat as the Valley League's perennial champions. It was no contest, and when he and Soapy left in the seventh, Curtis was leading, 8-1.

CHAPTER 8

The Big Challenge

RIP REDDING, Billy Jo, Rick Reilly, and Taps and Suzy Browning arrived exactly at 8:30 Friday morning, and six abreast, they started for the high school. Despite his trouble with Jerry Blaine, Chip's spirits were high. He had made a big step in enlisting the aid of Rip and Billy Jo, and he described the program to them with newfound enthusiasm.

As they approached the school, Chip saw Bill Sherman and a crowd of youngsters pointing to the windows of the building. Almost at the same instant, one of the boys saw him and called out, "Hey, Chip! Someone put graffiti on all the windows and walls."

Chip quickened his steps and stopped on the edge of the crowd. The windows and walls were covered with words and phrases crudely printed with chalk, soap, and what appeared to be white paint. There was a number of obscene words, and some of the phrases referred to the program and him.

"Baby-sitters," Rip read angrily, pointing to one of the windows.

"Nursery school athletes," Billy Jo added. "What's *that* all about?"

Chip scarcely heard them. Angry thoughts were running through his mind. Many hands had been engaged in this bit of work. Whose? The teenagers who hung out in front of the Sugar Bowl? Or had it been Jerry Blaine and his north-side gang?

The building superintendent's voice broke through his thoughts. "I've got to get some help. I'll never be able to clean this mess up by myself."

"We'll help," Chip said. He turned to the youngsters gathered around him. "How about it, gang?"

"Sure, Chip."

"You bet!"

"Let's go."

"We need buckets and brushes and rags and soap and water."

"We've got plenty of those," Sherman said. "Good thing they used whitewash instead of paint. It's gonna be a messy job any way you look at it. Some of you youngsters follow me." Turning, he led the way into the building, a half dozen boys and girls on his heels.

"It's a dirty trick, Chip," Billy Jo said gently. "I guess you're thinking it might be Jerry's work, but he wouldn't do anything like this. Speck would knock his block off."

"Billy Jo is right," Rip concluded. "I don't like to say it, but I wouldn't put it past some of the high school kids. It just seems more like them."

Sherman came back with the supplies and then departed to call Mayor Brooks. The youngsters started off strong enough; but it was a long, tiring job, and their enthusiasm gradually dwindled. Chip dismissed them and continued on with Rip, Billy Jo, Taps, and Suzy.

An hour later, Bill Sherman, accompanied by Mayor Brooks and Chief Burrows, arrived back on the scene.

Mayor Brooks was angry but not too upset to thank Chip and his companions for their help in cleaning up. After surveying the scene, he turned the investigation over to the police chief and left. "Don't forget the meeting tonight, Chip," he called over his shoulder.

Rip had to go to work at one o'clock, but Billy Jo stuck it out right through the day. When the job was finished, the kids had long since gone home. A feeling of guilt swept through Chip. He was being paid to do this job, but Billy Jo had worked as hard as if it had been *his* responsibility. *I'm not going to forget Billy Jo King for a long time,* he thought fiercely to himself.

Billy Jo seemed to sense Chip's thoughts. His friendly brown eyes were warm with understanding when he clasped Chip's hand. "I'll see you Monday morning," he said firmly.

After his new friend departed, Chip walked around to the back of the gymnasium. One phrase was still faintly visible: "Hilton's Baby-Sitting Club." He checked the gates and locked up. But he couldn't lock the phrase out of his mind. It rankled all the way home. He told his mother all about the vandalism while he ate a sandwich. After that, he showered, dressed quickly, and hustled downtown, arriving at the mayor's office at eight o'clock.

The doors of the outer and inner offices were open, and Mayor Brooks saw him walk in. "Come on in, Chip," he called. "You're right on time. We're meeting in the conference room tonight."

All the board members were present, and Chip nodded to them and took a seat at the large round cherry wood table. Brooks then called the meeting to order and asked Chip to give a report on the progress of the program. Chip opened his record book and read off the daily attendance. "We average about a hundred boys and girls a day," he said. "That's about it, except for the graffiti on the buildings."

"I knew something like that would happen," Hawkins said testily. "In fact, I said as much the first time we discussed this foolish program."

"No damage was done," Doc Jones said. "Why make such a fuss? Chip and his kids cleaned it up."

"The whole thing is a farce," Hawkins continued angrily. "All we've done is set up a baby-sitting club. In fact, I'm not too sure it's legal."

Brooks ignored him and turned to Chip. "I guess that's all, young man," he said gently. "You may be excused. Keep up the good work."

Chip thanked the mayor, nodded to the board members, and left the room. All of the members present, with the exception of Hawkins, nodded and said good night. The banker stared straight ahead, ignoring him completely.

Although several people spoke to him on the way home, Chip was too absorbed in thought to stop and speak to them. Incensed as he was at Henry Hawkins, he had to admit that the banker was right. With the exception of Rip Redding and Billy Jo King, he hadn't really made *any* progress in bringing the antagonistic factions together. Nor, he reflected soberly, had he made any progress with Mike Hogan. The burly superintendent of the tunnel project presented the biggest and most important aspect of all—he could provide jobs for everyone.

When Chip reached home, he told his mother he was tired and went straight to bed, but he couldn't get the "baby-sitting club" out of his mind. Why had Henry Hawkins used those precise words?

Saturday morning, Chip slept late, ate some cereal for breakfast, and started for the high school to watch the Colts workout. They were practicing when he arrived, and he sat down in the bleachers behind first base. Rip saw him and turned first base over to a tall youngster standing nearby.

"I've been watching for you," the high school star called as he approached. "Here," he said, reaching into his hip pocket. "I wrote out our lineup so you could look us over and know who we are." He handed the card to Chip, waited a moment, and then smiled when Chip nodded. "Tell us the truth now," he said, striding back to first base.

Chip scanned the list of names. He recognized the names of most of them, but with others his memory failed him. Two or three years made a difference when a fellow was growing up.

1	Ruiz, Thomas	2b
2	Hill, Keith	ss
3	Billy Jo	cf
4	Rip	1b
5	Green, Bob	lf
6	Gray, Jim	3b
7	Bender, Franco	rf
8	Lee, Hal	c
9	Baracat, Rick	p

He remained where he was during the fielding practice and for a time during batting practice. He made notes on the card and then shoved it in his pocket, waved good-bye to Rip and Billy Jo, and started home. On the way, he refreshed his memory reading the players' names again.

Jim Gray didn't have a strong enough arm to play third base, but Hal Lee, the catcher, had an exceptionally strong arm. If he were running the team, he would shift Ruiz to shortstop, Hill to second base, Lee to third base, Bender to left field, and Bob Green to right. That left the team without a catcher, but there had to be someone who could do a better job than Lee. It would be quite a shake-up, Chip reflected.

In the afternoon, he went back to the high school field to watch the Curtis-Valley Falls game. Slavin started on the mound for Curtis; Chip sat directly behind the lefty's receiver. He wanted to get a good look at the star pitcher's stuff.

It wasn't much of a contest. Slavin was taking it easy, almost toying with the batters, it seemed to Chip. During the four innings he pitched, the town team hitters could manage only a scratch hit, and Coach Curtis sent in another pitcher in the fifth inning. Curtis was leading 5-0 at this point, and Chip lost interest. His thoughts flashed back to the board meeting, and his chest tightened. What to do about the teenagers and the toughs . . .

He left the grandstand and was just passing through the main gate when he heard someone in the bleachers call his name. Even before he turned, he knew it was Soapy. The redhead leaped down from the top row of seats and came racing up to his side, grinning broadly.

"What are you doing here?" Chip asked.

"I quit."

"Quit! What do you mean?"

"I'm fed up with the house-making business. *And* Brighton! My Dad said I could take it easy and help out at home for the rest of the summer."

Sure, Chip was thinking. *Oh, sure.* Soapy knew Chip Hilton needed help. Well, it was no use to argue with Soapy. He was like that.

"Now I can help you with the recreation program," Soapy continued lightly.

"What about baseball? Didn't you sign up with Brighton?"

"Nope, I never did. Besides, they haven't played any games. I'm a free agent."

The redhead took off, and Chip continued at a leisurely pace on home. Soapy would be a tremendous help. He was full of fun, and the kids would be crazy about him. Somehow, his best pal always seemed to turn up when he needed him most. That was what friendship was all about, he reflected. At any rate, that was what it meant to Soapy Smith and Chip Hilton. Somehow, too, something good always seemed to follow when things appeared to be at their worst.

Sunday morning Chip went to church with his mom, and when she stopped to chat with the Smiths after the services, he joined Soapy.

"Good news," the redhead said excitedly. "Biggie and Speed and Red are home. We're coming over to your house after dinner. Around six o'clock. OK?"

"Of course! See you then," Chip promised.

On the way home, he was unusually quiet. His mom suggested he take a walk. "You've been surrounded by youngsters all week, and you haven't had a chance to think," she said gently.

"That's a good suggestion, Mom. I won't be long."

He walked down the hill, across the bridge, along the river road, and on toward the fairgrounds. His thoughts were circling continuously around what Doc had said about growing-ups handling grown-up problems. That was the key to everything. If he could only find a responsibility that the teenagers and older fellows could sink their teeth into, something big and challenging and tough and worthwhile . . . .

The way Billy Jo had pitched right in and assumed responsibility yesterday had proved the point.

Responsibilities were important to everyone. Without a challenge, there could be no responsibility. Where could he find a challenge?

Chip knew that was the weakness in the high school recreation program. There was no challenge for teenagers and older fellows. Chip was aware of an intangible but persistent thought that kept struggling for recognition, but he couldn't quite grasp it.

Between the road and the river he could see the fairgrounds. The sight brought back poignant memories. He would never forget the wonderful times he and the guys had enjoyed there. Even if some of the buildings were in bad shape, the grandstand and the racetrack were still in good condition, good enough for almost anything.

Then, slowly, it hit him.

There it was. Right before his eyes. The big challenge!

Why hadn't someone thought about converting the fairgrounds into a recreation park? Chip's heart leaped, and excited thoughts pounded through his brain. He had it at last! The project he had been searching for! It was big! Big enough and important enough to interest every person in Valley Falls: high school students, older teens, men, women, business people, politicians, and even Mike Hogan, the Tunnel Town giant.

One or two of the old buildings could be rehabilitated for rainy day programs. The rest could be torn down. Ball fields could be developed, basketball courts could be built, and the racetrack would be ideal for runners. With a few floats, the beach on the river, where he and the guys used to hang out, would be perfect for water sports.

Chip had the big idea!

He was seized with a feeling of exhilaration that made him want to yell and leap and turn somersaults.

HUNGRY HURLER

It could work! If he could get the town behind the project, hoping, trying, fighting—and praying—it could change Valley Falls!

CHAPTER 9

Baby-Sitting Club

"THE FAIRGROUNDS!" Mary Hilton repeated. "What about the fairgrounds?"

The words came tumbling out like the bounce, bounce, bounce of a basketball in the hands of an expert dribbler. "A Valley Falls recreation park, Mom. It would be a challenge for teenagers! A responsibility for older guys. There's plenty of room for basketball courts, tennis courts, soccer fields, and baseball fields. The racetrack could be used for running, and the river for swimming. Why, it will be a challenge for every person in Valley Falls—Tunnel Town too. *This* is the big thing Doc was talking about, something to pull all the factions in Valley Falls together. It's the perfect project to rebuild a sense of community!"

Mary Hilton shook her head doubtfully. "It's big, all right. Maybe too big. Chip. It would cost a fortune just to repair the buildings."

"We would only need one or two. Most of the rest of them could be torn down."

"A good fire would help," his mom said lightly. Then, noting the disappointment on his face, she continued gently. "I'm sorry, Chip. I just don't think you should rush headlong into this, son. What about the high school program? That's going well, isn't it?"

"It's fine for the little kids, but it isn't solving the problem. Rick and Taps and some of Rip Redding's friends can run that program. They love the responsibility."

Chip had no desire for food, and he ate only a few bites of Mary Hilton's scrumptious Sunday afternoon meal. His mind was besieged with a thousand exciting possibilities. After their meal, he helped his mom with the dishes and then sat down at the dining room table and drew out a map of the fairgrounds. He circled the buildings that he thought could be used and then marked off various sports areas. He was still at it around six o'clock when he heard Speed's Mustang roar into the driveway. Grabbing flashlights and dashing out of the house, he took the porch steps with one leap and cleared the white picket fence with another. "Don't unload," he cried. "Take off for the fairgrounds."

Speed started off and then turned his head. "Why the fairgrounds?" he asked.

"Inspection," Chip said quickly. "To see if it can be used for a recreation park."

"Recreation park?" Soapy repeated. "Can't be—the place is falling apart."

"Sure," Chip agreed. "That's the point. We wouldn't get it otherwise."

"What makes you think you *can* get it?"

"I can try."

They were approaching the grounds now, and Speed downshifted. His classic red fastback Mustang purred to a stop. Parking by the main gate, they unloaded, studied the low, one-story buildings for a time, and then made a slow tour of the grounds and the river.

Soapy and Speed were dubious, but they knew how much this meant to Chip.

After an hour or two of arguing and debating, they circled the property one more time, their flashlights playing across the overgrown field. Satisfied, the three friends headed to the Sugar Bowl for burgers and fries. Chip was suddenly ravenous. Biggie and Red joined them, and they returned to Chip's house and spent another hour preparing a master plan.

"Impossible," Red concluded when it was finished.

"It's got to be done," Chip said grimly.

"We thought the construction job was big," Biggie said, "but your problem is bigger. We've got to start back to Brighton. Ready, Soapy?"

"Not me. I'm home for the summer. You can drop me off at the house."

The guys piled into Speed's and Red's vehicles, and Soapy went along for the lift home. Chip spent the rest of the evening dreaming about the new venture and making plans. His mother headed up to bed around ten o'clock, but Chip was too excited to think of sleep. Later, when he could no longer keep his eyes open, he gave up and walked wearily to his room.

The next morning, he joined his mom for breakfast and then hurried down to Mayor Brooks's office. The outer door was open, and the administrator was seated at his desk. He beckoned to Chip and waved toward the familiar chair beside the desk.

"You're early," the mayor commented. "What's on your mind?"

Chip laid the master plan on the mayor's desk and carefully explained it. "We can give the town two things it needs badly, Mayor. A fine baseball field in front of the grandstand and a waterfront on the river."

"What about the racetrack?"

"It can be shortened and used for a running track."

"What about grass for the infield?"

"We can cut sod."

"Won't there be an element of danger in using the river for swimming?"

"Not with buoy lines and floats and lifeguards."

"Where are you going to get lifeguards?"

"I'm counting on the high school athletes."

Brooks studied Chip for a long moment. "You seem to have everything figured out," he said finally. "And I agree with you. The idea has tremendous possibilities."

Chip smiled and released a deep sigh. "That makes me feel better. If this doesn't pull everyone together, nothing will."

"Could be," Brooks said thoughtfully. "The physical plant is terribly run down. Fortunately, the water and electrical facilities have been kept in repair. You don't think you're biting off too much?"

"No, sir!"

"What's holding the teenagers and older boys back?"

"The very thing the fairgrounds will provide, sir. A challenge. A chance to do something big for the community. This project will be restricted to teenagers and older fellows. The younger kids' program will continue at the high school."

"What about Mike Hogan? I don't suppose you've come up with an idea that will swing him over. We need some jobs for our community. Badly."

Chip shook his head and smiled grimly. "No, sir, unfortunately I haven't any idea how to work that out. But I'm still thinking about it."

"How are you going to supervise all these activities?"

"I'll find the time. The high school students are helping a lot with the program there. Oh, by the way, do you have a map of the fairgrounds?"

"Better than that," Brooks said, rummaging in one of the drawers of his desk. "The fact is, I've got blueprints of everything—the water system, electrical wiring, sewage disposal. Here! Take them and figure it all out." He paused and then added hastily, "Not that I'm entirely sold on this, you understand."

Chip passed over that in a hurry. "Do you think the board will consider it?" he asked anxiously.

Brooks shook his head doubtfully. "They might," he said wryly. "The first thing we've got to do is clear it with John Schroeder."

"I'm glad you said *we*."

A quick smile shot across the mayor's lips. "You don't miss much, do you? Well, I don't anticipate any difficulty with John Schroeder, so I suppose the best thing is to plan a special meeting of the board for tomorrow night at eight o'clock. All right?"

"Perfect."

"You realize," Brooks continued ruefully, "that the board may give us quite a battle. Some of them will think you—we—are crazy."

"It's absolutely preposterous," Henry Hawkins said sarcastically. "You can't possibly be serious." He turned to the other board members.

"We're serious," John Schroeder said. "The high school program is a success, and I predict the recreation park idea will be even greater. I'm for it."

"What about supervision?" the banker managed. "How is Hilton going to supervise both places?"

"Chip explained that," Troll interrupted in a conciliatory tone of voice.

"Wasn't the *high school program* designed to attract the local teenagers and the north-side toughs?"

"Yes," Troll said quickly, "it was. We all know that. However, the program at the high school has been swamped with younger children. There's no room for older boys. Hilton's plan for the fairgrounds is perfect to meet the needs of the teenagers."

"You're right on one score," Hawkins retorted. "The high school program has attracted the children. My son ridicules the entire program. He says all the kids he knows call it Hilton's baby-sitting club."

"It was a splendid idea," Schroeder said calmly. "And it's up to us to decide whether or not we want to go a step further."

"You can decide it without my help," Hawkins said hotly. The angry man turned toward Doc Jones. "You cooked up the original deal to get a job for Hilton, and now you want to keep John Schroeder's property off the tax roll and have it improved at the town's expense. Pretty clever, I must say."

"The property has *never* been on the tax roll," Schroeder said coolly. "My family dedicated it to public use the first day it was acquired."

"I don't see what we have to lose," Troll offered.

"You can lose a member of this board," Hawkins said angrily, rising and striding out of the room.

There was a shocked moment of surprise following the banker's abrupt departure. A feeling of dismay swept through Chip. It seemed as if every suggestion he made led to trouble, to some kind of a crisis.

Mayor Brooks cleared his throat. "Henry's a little upset," he said softly. "But he isn't going to resign. He wouldn't have anything to gripe about or anyone to listen to him if he did. Let's get back to the business at hand. Would you like to put your opinion in the form of a motion, Dick?"

Troll made the motion, which passed unanimously. Chip's heart jumped. He had won!

"There you are, Chip," Brooks said. "You've got a green light. Keep in mind there's no money available. Do what you can. Even if you can build only a baseball field, it will be a start. We can budget part of the remainder next year."

The others nodded and left the room. Chip followed them down the steps and paused on the sidewalk. Then, for the first time, the enormousness of the undertaking struck home, and he felt a cold chill of apprehension. Why had he been so sure the fairgrounds project was the key to the town's problems? Besieged with doubts, he turned toward home.

Soapy was sitting in the swing on the porch when Chip turned the corner. Springing to his feet, the redhead leaped from the porch and raced toward him. "What happened?" he asked. "How did you make out?"

"All right. At least the board gave us permission to start."

"What about the buildings?"

"Most of them are to come down."

"You'll need a couple of bulldozers for that."

"Yes, and I know where to get them. Tunnel Town."

"Forget it," Soapy said. "From what I hear, Mike Hogan hates Valley Falls."

"I can try," Chip said, his spirits rising as he visualized the challenge. "After all, the Tunnel Town people stand to benefit from the park as much as anyone else. There must be some way to impress Mike Hogan."

Even as he spoke, Chip's mind was centering on the project superintendent. He had to win him over. But how? From what he had heard about the man, he knew Mike Hogan epitomized all the tunnel people: he was hard, proud, sure, strong, and self-reliant. Well, strong people liked direct action, and that was what Mike Hogan would get. "I'll see him first thing in the morning," he said decisively.

CHAPTER 10

Front-Page Feature

"MR. HOGAN?" Chip yelled, his voice barely rising above the pounding motors and the screech of the stream-powered elevator.

"You mean Mike Hogan? He's over there." A worker waved an arm toward a rough, unpainted building located just across the small creek, one of many that fed into the river. Chip waved thanks, crossed the shaky bridge above the sluggish stream, and opened the door of the shack.

The interior was as rugged as the exterior. The furniture had been constructed from rough lumber, and a reddish dust covered everything in sight: walls, tables, chairs, papers, and blueprints.

The field office was deserted except for one man. Chip would have known this was Mike Hogan no matter where he had met him. The word *big* described him perfectly. His massive head was perched above a bull neck that rested on wide, bulky shoulders. The short sleeves of the man's shirt displayed arms covered with bulging muscles. But when the big man looked up, it was his piercing blue eyes and the firm jaw that held Chip's attention.

Hogan glanced up from a blueprint he was studying, and his eyes shot appraisingly from Chip's face to his feet and back up again.

"Well?" he demanded. "What do you want?"

"I'd like to talk to you for a few minutes, Mr. Hogan."

"Well, talk!"

"My name is Chip Hilton. I'm in charge of the recreation program Valley Falls is sponsoring this summer."

Hogan stiffened in his chair, and the frown lines between his eyes deepened. "What about it?" he asked impatiently.

"I'd like to get some help."

"Help? What kind of help?"

"The use of some equipment to help develop a recreation park."

Hogan slowly let the air out of his massive lungs and leaned forward on the desk, his face expressing amazement. "You mean you want *me* to help you develop a recreation park for Valley Falls? Why, you must be crazy, boy! What has Valley Falls ever done for the people of Tunnel Town? Tell me. What?"

Before Chip could answer, the big man waved a hand toward the door. "I'm busy, young fellow. Too busy to talk to you and too busy to even think about Valley Falls, its recreation park, or its people. Close that door when you go out."

"I'll only be a few minutes—"

"Not with me, you won't. You won't be two seconds. I said get out. What part of 'get out!' don't you understand?"

Chip nodded. "I understand, sir, but—"

The words were wasted. Hogan had already turned back to his work and was busily examining blueprints. Closing the door behind him, Chip made his way across the makeshift bridge and walked slowly toward his mom's parked car. There was no doubt in his mind now about the depth of the wound that afflicted Mike Hogan. The man wanted no part of Valley Falls or anyone in the town.

As Chip threaded his way down the winding hill, he was deep in bitter thought. He sure hadn't made much progress! First, he had struck out with Jerry Blaine. Now with Mike Hogan. And despite his friendship with Rip and Billy Jo, he hadn't yet won over the high school teenagers. What next?

Well, he knew he had to keep at it. Chip made a mental to-do list. First, he would see Jim Butler at the *Sentinel* and give him the story on the fairgrounds project. He would visit with Petey Jackson next. Then he would join Rip and Billy Jo and the other guys at the high school and tell them the good news. Soapy would probably be there.

He would see Mr. Sherman and get the keys to the buildings at the fairgrounds and find out how to get the electricity and water working. Afterward, he and Soapy would work until it was time to go to the high school and watch the game between the Colts and Brighton.

He followed the schedule to the letter and eventually crossed off every item. The editor of the *Sentinel* was enthusiastic and promised to make the story a front-page feature. Rip, Billy Jo, Taps, Rick, and Suzy were all thrilled at the news.

Bill Sherman collected the keys and drove with him to the fairgrounds. He showed Chip how to turn on the water and electricity. Then they returned to the high school. Soapy was waiting for him. The two friends went home for a sandwich. Afterward, they rounded up a saw, hatchet, ax, pick, and shovel. Then, pocketing some fuses and a couple of light bulbs, they took off.

They worked until nearly six o'clock and then struck out for downtown. Chip dropped Soapy off on the corner of Main Street and then swung by the telephone company. His mom was just walking down the steps as Chip pulled into the parking lot.

At home, Chip showered while his mom prepared dinner. Later, when he arrived at the high school field, the game was already in the fourth inning. He glanced quickly at the scoreboard. Brighton was at bat and leading 7-0.

A small gathering of local teenagers was in the grandstand, but they had little to cheer about. In fact, they were showing their displeasure by booing the Colts players and showering them with sarcastic words of advice. Soapy was sitting directly behind home plate, and Chip joined him.

"No contest," the redhead said. "Colts can't get them out."

After the third out, two more runs appeared on the scoreboard, and the Brighton manager began substituting. Biggie, Speed, and Red left the game and came tramping up into the grandstand. They sat down beside Chip and Soapy and relaxed. "How did we look?" Biggie asked.

"It didn't really look like you were playing anyone," Soapy observed.

"Then why don't you help them out?" Speed asked. "They sure could use a catcher."

"And some pitching," Red added.

"Well," Soapy drawled, "Chip and I might just follow your advice. If we do, the Colts will be playing Curtis for the championship a month from today."

"Don't forget it's double elimination," Speed said. "One more loss and they're through as far as the championship is concerned."

"How can they lose with me behind the plate?" Soapy demanded.

The last remark started one of the verbal sparring matches Soapy and Speed loved to engage in, and it lasted until the end of the game. "We're going right back to Brighton," Biggie explained as they got up to leave. "See you guys Sunday."

Chip and Soapy walked slowly away from the field toward home, discussing the Colts players and possible changes that might help.

"We've got to do something for them," Chip said worriedly. "Rip and Billy Jo didn't hold back when I needed *their* help."

When they reached the house, Mary Hilton came out to meet them on the porch. "Rip Redding called," she said. "He wanted to know if you were going to be home. He said he and Billy Jo King would be along shortly."

Half an hour later, Rip and Billy Jo walked up on the porch and sat down on the top step without a word. After a long moment, Rip looked up at Chip. "Hope you don't mind," he said apologetically. "We *had* to talk to someone."

"Are you kidding?" Chip said quickly. "We know exactly how you feel. In fact, we've been talking about you and Billy Jo and the team. We were thinking we might be able to help."

"You mean, play with us?" Billy Jo asked excitedly.

"Sure, if you'll have us."

"Have you?" Rip said. "Oh, man! Would we ever! You know something? The team wanted me to ask you to manage us. That's why we're here."

"You mean we can't play?"

"Now I know you're kidding," Billy Jo laughed.

"Nope," Chip said firmly, "we're not. We'll play. However, you've got to do something for us in return."

"Name it!" Rip said quickly.

"The players have to help with the fairgrounds work, and Billy Jo has to get some of the guys from the north side to do the same thing."

Rip and Billy Jo looked at each other for a brief second, their faces expressing amazed delight. They sprang to their feet and waltzed around the porch. Stopping suddenly, they extended their hands. "Let's shake on it," they said in unison.

All four of them clasped hands and then they went in the house to the family room to firm up the practice times and make a few changes in the team.

"You're the boss," Rip said happily.

"Right!" Billy Joe said. "First thing tomorrow we're going to put you both on the roster."

"Oh, boy!" Rip said. "Have we got a club now. With Soapy catching and you pitching, we'll clean up the league."

"Wait a second," Chip said quickly, holding up his hand. "I didn't say anything about pitching. I'll manage the team and play in the outfield or some place, but it's going to take me a little time to get in shape to pitch."

"Whatever you say," Rip said expansively. "You're in charge."

In charge he was! And with a full crew. When he and Soapy reached the fairgrounds Thursday morning, they found Rip and Billy Jo waiting. And they weren't alone. Several of the Colts players were with them, and Billy Jo had brought along a dozen or more north-siders as well. They were equipped with picks and shovels and hoes—ready to work. And they meant business. They worked until noon, left for lunch, and were back in the afternoon. By evening, the area in front of the grandstand was cleared, the racetrack fence had been dismantled, and an infield was laid out.

"We'll hold Colts practice here tomorrow evening," Chip said elatedly. "Six o'clock. Pass the word."

The work crew came back again on Friday, and by five o'clock the infield was lined and ready for practice. Chip left Rip, Billy Jo, and Soapy in charge and took off for the weekly board meeting. His spirits were soaring at the progress they had made.

All the board members were present with the exception of Henry Hawkins. Chip told them about the help he was getting from the Colts and the northsiders, and as much as he disliked discouraging them, he related the reception he had received in his encounter with Mike Hogan.

"Par for the course," Doc growled.

"We're not giving you much help," Troll said.

"I'll be around again when I need it," Chip said, smiling. "Oh! Would it be all right to let the Colts call the fairgrounds ball field their home field?"

"I don't know why not," Brooks said. "After all, you're in charge and they're helping to build it."

Chip got up early Saturday morning and drove straight to the fairgrounds. An hour later, Soapy's father dropped the redhead off, and the rest of the workers appeared soon afterward. They plugged away until noon when Chip thanked them and gave them the afternoon off. "See you Monday morning?" he asked.

"You got it, Chip!"

"Right!"

"It's looking pretty good, isn't it, Chip?"

"We'll be here. Who would've thought we could do something like this!"

On the way home, he stopped off at Mama Trullo's bakery and deli and ordered two Italian subs for lunch. When he reached home, his mom was gardening. "Come on, Mom!" Chip called. "I've got Mama Trullo's subs!" While they were devouring the delicious sandwiches, Mary Hilton told Chip to read the paper. "Read the first page," she said proudly.

Jim Butler had been true to his word. A big streamer headed three columns on the right side of the first page, a space usually reserved for important local news.

VALLEY FALLS RECREATION PARK TO BE DEVELOPED
Town Commissioners Approve Plan

Mayor Brooks announced last Wednesday morning that the board of commissioners has approved conversion of the fairgrounds to a recreation park. Chip Hilton, serving as Valley Falls's first summer recreation director, was the motivating force behind the project. Mayor Brooks stated that the town board stands solidly behind him in its development.

Hilton says the fairgrounds program will stress activities for teenagers and young men and women. Interested persons are urged to donate their personal services to this worthwhile community project.

"The town council certainly has confidence in you, Chip," his mother said, her voice filled with pride.

"That's why I've got to make the recreation park a success, Mom."

"You will," she said confidently. "By the way, there's something on the next page about your coaching and playing for the Colts baseball team. I had hoped you would take a rest from sports for awhile."

FRONT-PAGE FEATURE

Chip turned the page quickly, and his heart dropped like a poorly skipped stone in a pool of water. "Oh, no," he murmured.

CHIP HILTON—SOAPY SMITH: NEW COLT BATTERY

The *Sentinel* learned yesterday that Chip Hilton and Soapy Smith, State University's star battery, have been added to the Colts roster. Hilton has been named team manager and is slated to face Tunnel Town at 2:30 P.M., Saturday, July 20, at the high school field. It will be the all-American's first appearance in a Colts uniform and in the Valley Falls area in several years.

CHAPTER 11

Still in the Race!

TENSION ELECTRIFIED the air on Monday morning. Although the sky was clear and bright, the atmosphere was charged as if by an electrical storm. Rip Redding's Colts were on hand as were a number of north-siders. There was a new addition too. The boy Chip had helped, Michael, was standing in front of the grandstand surrounded by several other teenagers.

Chip quickly made the work assignments and then went over to talk to Michael. Motioning him to one side, he shook hands with the good-looking boy. "I'm glad to see you. I guess you got home all right."

The boy nodded. "I wanted to thank you."

"Forget it," Chip said quickly. "I'm helping manage the Colts, and we're practicing here every afternoon. Why don't you work out with us?"

Michael shook his head. "Oh, no, I couldn't. I'm not good enough."

"You're as good as any pitcher we have. Besides, Rip Redding has already put your name on the roster."

The boy's face blanched. "No!" he managed. "You can't do that."

"Why not?"

"My father is . . . well, my last name is Hogan."

Thoughts were racing through Chip's mind. Of course! He should have realized that the night he had the fight with Blaine. "Hogan!" he said. "You mean Mike Hogan is your father?"

Michael's eyes dropped. Then his glance shifted swiftly upward, and he eyed Chip steadily. "Yes, he is," the boy said firmly.

"What's that got to do with playing baseball?"

"Not playing ball, but playing with a Valley Falls team."

"All right," Chip said briskly, "forget the team. You can still practice with us though. I'll work with you every day just the way I do with the other pitchers. Only thing is, you'll have to wear a Colts uniform. All right?"

Michael's eyes brightened, and he nodded eagerly. "I'll say! I'd better get to work now. Thanks, Chip."

Chip called off the work details at four o'clock that afternoon and began the practice session. While the others were busy with batting practice, Chip and Soapy took Rick Baracat, Franco Bender, and Michael to one side and worked on their pitching.

A little later Soapy took over the pitchers while Chip started infield practice. Some of the Colts were working at odd jobs and reported late, but Chip gave each a chance. It was nearly dark when the last player departed, but Chip and Soapy remained at the field another half-hour discussing each player's strengths and weaknesses.

The rest of the week was spent in developing the ball field and waterfront, and in working with the Colts team. Chip's spirits rose as the team steadily improved and the game with Tunnel Town drew closer.

Friday evening, after all the Colts had gone home, he sat down in front of the grandstand and breathed a happy sigh. "They're ready, Soapy," he said confidently.

"You wouldn't know it was the same team if it weren't for the uniforms," Soapy agreed.

"Especially with you doing the catching."

"Well," Soapy said darkly, "you better dig up a couple more hurlers. These kids want to win. So do I!"

"You don't think I want to lose, do you?" Chip asked.

Soapy glared at him for a moment. "You'd better start doing some throwing then," he said gruffly. "I wonder if Michael will come to the game?"

"Of course. I'm sure he'll want to watch his brother play."

Soapy grunted. "Are you kidding? Chip, he couldn't care less. He told me they never speak. Same with his father."

"It's hard to understand. The kid needs game experience, and he's missing his big chance this summer."

"Well," Soapy said wearily, rising to his feet, "let's go home. We've done all we could do in a week. And, if we lose tomorrow, it will be over. The Colts will be out of it, and we can sit back and root for the guys and Brighton."

"We're not going to lose, Soapy," Chip assured him. "I'll meet you at the high school at twelve o'clock tomorrow."

Chip went to bed early that night and met Soapy at the field at noon. The game wasn't scheduled to begin until three, but Chip wanted to be sure the Colts got a thorough pregame workout. Around one o'clock, the Tunnel Town team arrived, and a little later he spotted

Michael in the grandstand. The youngster was surrounded by several of his buddies and was hunched down in his seat as if he wanted to keep out of sight.

When hitting and fielding practice was over, both teams huddled in front of their respective dugouts. Out on the diamond the umpire was dusting off home plate. Then he turned and announced the Colts battery. Chip had selected Rick Baracat to start on the mound with Soapy behind the plate.

Soapy walked slowly along beside Rick all the way out to the mound, talking earnestly to the youngster and trying to give him confidence. Then the redhead turned and swaggered back to the plate and took Rick's warm-up throws.

Their first time at bat, the Tunnel Town players didn't look like much of a team. They did hit the ball, but Baracat had superb support. Rip fielded a hard-hit grass cutter and made the play at first all alone for the first out. The second batter flied out to Billy Jo, and the third hitter popped up. Jim Gray, playing third base, gathered in the fly ball for the third out.

The Colts couldn't score in their half of the first inning, and that was the tempo of the game for the first five innings. Neither team could bunch its hits, but both were playing good defensive ball.

Chip had recognized Michael's brother while the visitors were taking their fielding practice. Bill Hogan looked just like his father and was nearly as big. He was doing the catching for the visitors. During batting practice he consistently banged out long fly balls, but, so far in the game, he hadn't been able to buy a hit.

Rick Baracat had good control but little else, and although Tunnel Town was hitting freely, the ball always seemed to go straight at a Colts fielder. In the bottom of the sixth, the Colts managed to move a run across the plate for the first score. Their 1-0 lead didn't last long.

Tunnel Town came right back in the top of the seventh and scored three runs. In the eighth, the Colts scored twice to tie up the game. Chip breathed a sigh of relief.

His relief was short-lived. In the top of the ninth, Tunnel Town scored twice to take a 5-3 lead. *It's now or never for the Colts,* Chip thought.

They came running in full of pep and still fighting. Chip took a quick look at the book. Billy Jo was up next. Chip patted him on the back and told him to look them over. "Get on," he said. "We'll bring you in."

Billy Jo did just that, bringing the Colt fans to their feet by driving a Texas leaguer to deep right and going into second base standing up. Rip Redding followed with a single to left field, and Billy Jo barely beat the fielder's throw to third base. The tying run was now on first base with none away.

Bob Green was up, but he hadn't touched the ball in three tries at bat. He didn't do it now either, going down on three straight strikes.

One away!

That brought up Jim Gray. The stocky third baseman worked the count to three-and-two and then cut under the ball and was out on an easy fly ball to the first baseman. Billy Jo was still anchored at third and Rip had been unable to advance.

Two away!

It was now or never, and while Chip was debating the Colts's next move, Rip Redding called time and made the decision for him. Getting permission from the umpire, he came trotting into the dugout. "What do you say, Chip? We need you now. Hal won't mind."

"I sure won't," Hal offered quickly, moving back from the on-deck circle. "This is no time for me to bat."

It was a show-off situation, the kind Chip shied away from, but he knew he had no choice. "All right, Rip," he said quickly. "I'll try."

Rip trotted over to the umpire, made the substitution, and hurried back to first base. Billy Jo, standing at third base, grinned across at Chip and nodded his head confidently as the fans came to their feet.

"Hilton batting for Lee."

It was only a small crowd, but from the clamor that followed the announcement, it reminded Chip of the roar of the fans at the disastrous championship game when he slid home to tie up the score. Soapy followed him almost to the plate, a bat in his hand.

"Save me a turn," the redhead pleaded. "I'll bring you all in."

Chip stopped on the first-base side of the plate for a second and looked at Billy Jo. Then he nodded toward Rip and flashed the sign for the steal. Just to make sure there would be no mistake, he gave the sign again. He had to get Rip safely down to second base.

It was a dangerous play and a tough decision. He knew the Tunnel Town players would probably be expecting it, but if he could get Rip down to second, any kind of a hit had a chance of bringing him home to tie up the score. Besides, Rip was fast and knew how to hit the dirt.

Chip stepped into the batter's box, noting that the infielders were playing deep and thinking only about the third out. The pitcher came in with a sharp curve that broke down toward Chip's knees. Chip stepped forward and took a full cut at the ball, trying for a miss, hoping to hamper the catcher's throw to second base.

Rip was away on the pitch, tearing out for second base while Billy Jo paused a few feet off third base. The catcher made the throw, but Rip was ahead of the ball, and the second baseman ran forward and met the peg seconds too late. Now the tying run was on second, and it was up to Chip to bring it in.

Bill Hogan suddenly called time. Pulling off his mask, he held a short consultation with the pitcher. Then the pitcher threw four straight balls wide of the plate, and Chip trotted down to first.

It was the last of the ninth, with two down, the bases loaded, and two runs behind.

The fans were yelling and stamping their feet, and Soapy loved it! He swaggered up to the plate and got set in the righty batter's box. Now the pressure was on the Tunnel Town players! Soapy started to play cat and mouse with the pitcher, stepping out of the box and back in again until the exasperated umpire began to get angry and ordered him up to the plate.

The count went from one-and-nothing to one-and-one, two-and-two, and finally three-and-two—the full count.

The pitcher delivered, and Billy Jo, Rip, and Chip took off. Chip heard the crack of the bat on the ball and saw the backpedaling left fielder suddenly turn and sprint for the fence. There was nothing more to see so he sped on around second. Then, out of the corner of his eye, he saw Billy Jo cross the plate and Rip turn third base.

Now he really poured it on, sprinting for all he was worth toward the hot corner. Up ahead, Franco Bender's head was moving from left to right and back again, his eyes measuring the length of the throw and the distance to home plate. That was enough for Chip! He kept right on going, turned third, and sprinted for home.

Bill Hogan was planted solidly in front of the plate, waiting for the throw. It was going to be close. Ten feet away, Hogan shifted his glove slightly to the right, and

Chip left the ground, diving headlong into the big catcher. They crashed to the ground in a tangle of legs and arms and gritty dust. Chip's hand shot forward and found the plate a split second before the gloved ball thumped into his back.

"Safe!"

Chip scrambled to his feet, his thoughts racing. He had scored the winning run, and Soapy Smith had made it all possible. Now the Colts could look ahead to Bradford, Clarksville, Brighton, and Curtis. And, he added to himself, Lefty Slavin.

He turned to look for Soapy. His pal was loping along from third base, waving his arms in the air and yelping in delight. Chip went to meet him. He never made it. Kids came from everywhere, it seemed, and surrounded the redhead. They had Soapy on their shoulders in wild celebration. Then the Colts were on him, thumping him on the back, rubbing his head, and yelling as madly as the kids.

The Colts were still in the race!

CHAPTER 12

Colts Go-Go Club

GO, COLTS! Yeah, Chip! Yeah, Rip! Hurray, Billy Jo! Three cheers for Soapy!

The signs were printed and scribbled on old sheets, tablecloths, cardboard, and poster paper, and they were hanging on the fence of the high school field, the building itself, and on the telephone poles on the street.

Chip and Soapy paused in happy silence to look at the display, and then they saw the young kids peering out at them from behind the bleachers. A second later the fans came charging out. Rip, Billy Jo, Taps, Rick, and Suzy, surrounded by the young boys and girls, were grinning broadly as the boys and girls all talked at once.

"You like the signs?"

"We formed a Colts booster club."

"We call it the Colts Go-Go Club."

"All right with you?"

"Great! Just great," Chip told them. "You are right on the ball. And that reminds me. Soapy and I have to get busy at the fairgrounds. We'll see you all later! Let's go, Soapy."

When they reached the fairgrounds, a number of the Colts players were already there. There were some new faces in the crowd, too, and Chip sensed a new feeling of enthusiasm.

Everyone pitched in and worked hard all day to level and grade the field. It was pick, shovel, and wheelbarrow work—tough going—but no one complained. When Chip called it a day, the infield was beginning to shape up. Later, the Colts assembled for the afternoon workout. Michael Hogan, dressed in one of the old Colts uniforms, joined them. Chip spent a great part of the afternoon working with the pitchers. All of them were showing improvement, but Michael's progress was almost unbelievable.

Soapy called early Tuesday morning to say he had to help his father all day. "I'll see you first thing tomorrow," he promised.

Chip checked in with Taps, Suzy, and Rick on the program at the high school and then went over to the fairgrounds. This time, there were only a few Colts players on site, and the work program dragged. Later that evening, after everyone had left, Chip locked up the tools and started for home. Then, on a sudden impulse, he decided to stop by Billy Jo's house for a chat.

As he approached the house, he saw a group of boys hanging out in front of Murdock's. They spotted him at the same time and watched curiously when he turned in at Billy Jo's. Billy Jo's brother again opened the door. This time, the boy recognized him.

"He isn't home, Chip," Little Jo said. "He's washing Doc Jones's car."

Chip thanked the young boy and continued on along the street. As he approached the store, talk stopped, but several boys spoke to him. Two blocks farther on, he saw the bridge and noted several figures leaning against the stone wall at the entrance. The corner light was on, and as he drew nearer, he could see that these were older teenagers.

Then his heart leaped. Jerry Blaine and the two men who had been with him the night of the trouble at the bus station were in the center of the group. One of them turned toward Chip and then swung quickly back to Jerry, saying something in a low voice. Then, just as Chip came abreast of the group, the three of them closed ranks in front of him. It was the same maneuver they had used to halt Petey at the bus station.

"Where're all your pals?" Jerry said insolently. "Don't you know it's dangerous to roam around over here all alone?"

"No, I don't," Chip said evenly, starting to walk around the group. "Anyway, the team didn't practice this evening." On an impulse Chip added, "Why don't some of you guys come out for the Colts team?"

"You must be kidding," Jerry exclaimed. "Now, if you invited us down to the fairgrounds for a fight, we'd all come. But to play baseball with the high school punks, uh-uh. Besides, right now you and me have a personal score to settle."

"I have no reason to fight."

"I'm gonna give you one."

"No, you're not!" a voice said quickly, behind Chip. "Leave Chip alone. He's Billy Jo's friend."

"You keep out of this, Little Jo," Jerry said roughly.

Chip turned to see Billy Jo's little brother and a dozen other boys of assorted sizes. He recognized some of them as the teenagers who had been standing in front of Murdock's. There seemed to be two factions in the group, but Little Jo had the most support.

"No," Little Jo said firmly. "I won't. And I'm going to tell Billy Jo as soon as he comes home."

"Yeah," another boy said. "Billy Jo said Chip Hilton's a good guy. Besides, he's fixing up a place for us to play and swim and that's more 'n you ever did for any of us."

It wasn't clear what might have happened if there had not been still another interruption. He heard running footsteps as someone called, "Jerry! Quick! You gotta help."

"Turk!" Jerry shouted. "What's wrong?"

"Speck is on one of his binges," the runner gasped. "He's beating up everybody in the house."

Turk started running back in the direction from which he had come farther up the hill, and Jerry and the others followed, evidently forgetting all about the fight. Chip paused uncertainly for a moment, and without stopping to reason why, took off at full speed to catch up with them.

The house was less than a block away. As Chip approached, he could see men, women, and children standing on the sidewalk looking up at the house. There was a light on in every room, and the front door was standing open. No one had made a move to go in the house. Turk and Jerry stopped at the bottom of the long flight of stone steps leading up to the porch.

An obviously urgent plea for help came from the house. Turk grasped Jerry by the arm and tried to urge him up the steps. "Let's go!" he cried.

"Nothing doing," Jerry said angrily, flinging Turk's hand away. "I'm not going to tangle with him when he's like this."

Another scream was suddenly choked off, and Chip waited no longer. He took the steps two at a time, crossed the porch with two long strides, and entered the hall. He could hear scuffling in the second room on the right. He hurried along the hall and turned in at the doorway.

The room was in shambles. A table had been upset and chairs were strewn around the room. In the center of the room, Speck Blaine was barefoot and wearing nothing but a pair of sweatpants. He was trying to choke a girl. Her hair was disheveled, and there was a long scratch across her face. Speck's back was to Chip. Chip sprang forward, slipped his hands under Speck's arms, and tried to apply a full nelson.

Speck's body was wet with sweat, and Chip couldn't lock his fingers; but he did manage to pull the man away from the girl. "Run!" Chip yelled to the girl. "Go out the front door. Leave it open."

The girl flashed a frantic look in Speck's direction and dashed for the door. Speck was straining with maniacal fury now, and it was only a matter of seconds until he would free himself. Chip swung him to one side suddenly, pulled his arms free, and gave Speck a hard push.

Turning, he dashed down the hall toward the front door with Speck in full pursuit. The man was right on his heels. Chip grabbed the door and slammed it shut. He held on to the knob and kept pulling on the door, expecting Speck to try and open it.

Suddenly, there was a terrible crash and a shower of glass as Speck hurled his hands and arms forward through the glass panel in an attempt to grab Chip. But then Speck seemed to disappear. Except for Chip's pounding heart and Speck's heavy breathing, there was silence.

Trying to regain his breath, Chip stood there and waited for Speck's next move. Suddenly, he saw a little trickle of blood seep under the door and spread slowly on the floor of the porch. He did not grasp its meaning for a long moment. Then it hit him, and he forced the door—and Speck's body—slowly back.

Speck was lying on the floor staring uncomprehendingly at the flow of blood coming from each of his wrists. All the wrath and fury had drained out of the man. Chip grasped him under the arms and dragged him to a couch. At the same time, the girl, Turk, and Jerry crowded through the door.

"Quick!" Chip called, "Get something to make a tourniquet. I need two!"

All three ran toward the kitchen. Meanwhile, Chip held Speck's forearms, clamping each wrist with a thumb directly above the cuts. The girl was back in a moment with a clean dish towel. Turk and Jerry followed and stood beside the couch watching as she tore the towel into strips. Chip tied them around Speck's forearms just above the wrists. The girl went back to the kitchen, returning a moment later with two clothespins that Chip used as keys to tighten the tourniquets.

"We need a doctor," Chip said urgently, looking at Jerry.

Jerry shook his head. "You won't get anyone to come here."

"I can get someone," Chip said. "Here! Hold these tourniquets."

He called Doc Jones and reached him at his home. The physician wanted to know what Chip had done and how seriously Speck was injured. Chip explained that Speck's wrists were badly cut. Doc Jones said he would be right along and would call 9-1-1 for an ambulance too.

Meanwhile, Speck's mother came down the stairs. She went into the kitchen for a pan and some cold water and bathed Speck's face and arms. Speck, who was only partly in possession of his faculties, didn't remember what had happened.

It was an awkward situation, and Chip was glad when he heard a car stop in front of the house. A moment later Doc Jones strode up on the porch closely followed by Billy Jo. Doc examined Speck's wrists and adjusted the tourniquets. While he was working, the ambulance arrived, and two attendants entered the house carrying a stretcher.

"Good work, Chip," Doc said. "Let's get him down to the ambulance."

"Will he be all right?" Mrs. Blaine asked, grasping Doc's arm.

"Yes, Mrs. Blaine," Doc said gently. "Thanks to Chip Hilton."

Billy Jo and Jerry helped the attendants carry Speck down the steps in the stretcher and place him in the ambulance. Doc followed them. The boy, Turk, grasped Chip's arm and murmured his thanks.

"I won't forget what you did," he said in a low voice.

"I'm glad I could help," Chip said gently. "He's a strong man."

They had reached the bottom of the steps, and the onlookers were pressing close to get a look at Speck. Many of them were nodding toward Chip and speaking in low tones. As the ambulance drove away, Doc grasped Chip by the arm and walked him along the sidewalk.

Looking around to be sure they were far enough away to avoid being overheard, he spoke in a low voice. "This could be the break you've been looking for, and you've got to exploit it. I'll have a long talk with Speck while I've got him on his back and see if we can't get his support. Drop in at the office around nine o'clock in the morning. I just might have something interesting to report."

He walked back with Doc to his car and rejoined Billy Jo and the two brothers. With the exception of

Jerry's friends and the kids, the crowd had melted away. Jerry and Turk said nothing and Billy Jo broke the tense silence by saying he would walk along with Chip to the bridge. Jerry nodded, and he and Turk turned away without a word.

"They appreciated what you did, Chip," Billy Jo said, "but they didn't know how to thank you."

"No thanks were necessary, Billy Jo. I would have done the same thing for anyone."

"I know," Billy Jo said. "It's hard for us to grasp that idea, but I believe you."

They parted at the bridge, and Chip continued home, his thoughts racing ahead to the next morning. Speck, as the north-side leader, exercised just as much power in his neighborhood as Mike Hogan did in Tunnel Town. *He is a strong link,* Chip breathed. He might not win over everyone, but tomorrow he would meet with Speck.

CHAPTER 13

A Homer in Any Park

CHIP JOGGED down to Doc Jones's office above the Sugar Bowl at 8:30 the next morning. The outer office was unlocked, as usual. He went in and sat down to wait, restlessly leafing through the magazines on the coffee table. Chip had experienced a sleepless night and he was on edge. Then he heard Doc's heavy steps on the stairs and rushed to meet the physician. "What happened?" he asked.

"Everything in due time," Doc said calmly. The physician unlocked his inner office and motioned Chip to a chair. He placed his old leather case on a table, took off his hat, and sat down behind the desk. "Well," he said, "Speck is in pretty good shape, everything considered. I had a long talk with him this morning—not that I made much of an impression, as far as I could see."

Chip's hopes sank. *I expected too much*, he told himself. Speck Blaine wasn't the type to break down just because he was hurt.

"But," Doc continued, "I certainly haven't given up hope. He wants to talk to you this afternoon. Two o'clock."

Thanking his old friend, Chip assured the doctor that he would meet him at the hospital. Then he started out for the high school. He arrived just as his helpers were assembling the kids in the grandstand. Soapy saw him and rushed up. "Billy Jo told us about last night," he said. "How's Speck?"

Billy Jo came up in time to hear the question. "Never mind Speck," he said. "How are *you?*"

Chip grinned and said he was just fine. He told them about his meeting with Doc and his scheduled visit at the hospital that afternoon. "It could mean a lot," he concluded. "Speck could swing every person on the north side."

"You're right about that, Chip," Billy Jo agreed. "He's like the mayor in our part of town."

Chip sent Soapy and Billy Jo over to the fairgrounds and then helped the high school staff with the kids until it was time for them to go home to lunch. It was five minutes to two o'clock when Chip arrived at Valley Falls Hospital. A volunteer in the lobby gave him Speck Blaine's room number and directed Chip to the bank of elevators against the far wall.

He took the elevator to the third floor. The door to Speck's room was closed, but he could hear voices inside. He knocked, and Doc Jones's voice rang out, telling him to come in. To Chip's surprise, Speck was sprawled in a chair beside a small desk with both his arms bandaged to the elbows. Doc was sitting in the only other chair. Jerry and Turk were leaning against the bed.

"Speck," Jones said, "this is Chip Hilton."

Speck looked at him steadily for a moment. "Hiya, Hilton," he said. "Glad to see you. Now, Doc, Jerry,

Turk, if you don't mind, I'd like to talk to Hilton alone. Don't go too far away though."

Doc got up, opened the door, motioned Turk and Jerry to precede him, and then followed the two boys, closing the door softly behind them.

As soon as the door closed, Speck got to his feet and extended his bandaged right hand. "I want to shake your hand, Hilton. Doc Jones says you saved my life. He said you helped me when even my own kin was afraid to. I figure I owe you something, a favor."

"I could sure use it," Chip said, grasping Speck's hand gently.

"Name it."

"You could help stop the fighting between the north-siders and the high school boys."

Speck thought that over for a moment. "That would be a switch," he said, his eyes twinkling, "me putting a ban on fightin." He mused aloud. "Yes, that idea kind of appeals to me. All right, maybe I can do just that."

Chip opened the door, and Doc and the two boys filed back in. Doc smiled at Speck and nodded. "You remember him now, eh? Remember when he used to play on the high school teams?"

Speck nodded. "Sure. I remembered him before that. I used to see him down at the fairgrounds. Most of the time he would be down there playing ball or practicing by himself if there was no one else around." He sized Chip up and added, "You're a lot bigger than you were in those days."

"He's a lot bigger in sports too," Turk said.

"I know," Speck said shortly, "I read the papers." He deliberated a moment and continued, "Sure! Hilton got big in sports because he worked at it." He glared at his brothers for a long second. "Why can't you two birds do the same thing?"

"Billy Jo King says they're good ballplayers," Chip interjected. "The Colts need players. They ought to come out for the team."

"All right," Speck said. "They'll be there. Count on 'em."

"But Speck—" Jerry began to protest.

"Don't you 'Speck' me! You get down to the fairgrounds this afternoon. You, too, Turk. You hear?"

"Yes, Speck. I hear."

Speck looked over at Chip. "See if you can teach these two some baseball, Hilton. If they give you any trouble, let me know. Oh, yes," he said, turning back to Jerry. "I heard about the fight you and those bosom pals of yours had with Hilton, and I don't want to hear of it happening again. Not you and not anyone else from the north side."

He got up from his chair and walked over to the bed. "Now, everybody get out of here. I want to get some sleep."

Chip led the way to the elevator. He pressed the button and tried to think of something to say. He *had* to say something. "I guess you know I've been managing the Colts," he said to the others.

Turk nodded. "Sure," he said, "everyone knows that."

The elevator arrived, and they got in. Chip wanted to keep the conversation going. As the door closed he said, "We need players badly. What positions do you play?"

"I play second base," Turk said quickly. "Jerry can catch or play in the outfield. He's a good hitter."

Jerry grunted. "Only in pickup ball," he said scornfully.

It was the first time he had spoken, and Chip was quick to take advantage of the opportunity to keep him talking. "That's where I started. That's where a player learns the most."

"Neither of us ever had any coaching," Jerry said lamely. "We just played for fun."

"We play for fun, but we play to win too."

The elevator arrived at the main floor, and they walked out through the hall and paused on the porch. Chip had been trying to think of a way to soften the orders Speck had given to Jerry. Suddenly, he had it. "We start practice at four o'clock," he said. "Why don't you come along with Billy Jo? I'll tell him to meet you at Murdock's. OK?"

"Sure," Turk said. "We'll be ready."

Chip left them standing on the porch and took the shortcut along the river to the fairgrounds. Soapy and Billy Jo met him at the gate, and Chip told them about Speck's decision. Both immediately grasped the importance of the situation, and Billy Jo said he would be happy to escort the Blaine brothers to practice.

"I'm on my way as we speak," Billy Jo said. "This is *one* time I'll be glad to see Jerry Blaine. Guess I'll head up there now."

Michael Hogan was working with the crew that day. Chip called him aside and related the events of the past two hours. "Try not to talk about this thing, Michael. It will probably be awkward for Jerry too. All right?"

"Sure, Chip. I won't say anything to him."

He was throwing to the hitters when he saw Billy Jo approaching with Jerry and Turk. All three wore baseball caps, T-shirts, baseball pants, long socks, and sneakers.

Chip didn't waste any time on introductions. There wasn't a person on the field who didn't know Jerry and Turk. He waved to the three north-siders and sent them to the outfield to shag flies. Twenty minutes later, he called the outfielders in for their turns at bat and sent Franco Bender to the mound to throw. The batters got their gloves and ran out on the field. It was the first time Jerry and Turk had joined up with any of the Colts in a huddle, but Chip passed it over lightly. "Turk," he said, "you lead off; Keith, next; Billy Jo; Jim; and then Jerry. I'll hit last. Take three hits and a bunt and run it out. We'll go around three times and then have fielding practice."

Turk was nervous but eager. Even so, he made Franco Bender put the ball over the plate. He met each pitch solidly, and, on the bunt, took off for first base like a streak. Keith, Billy Jo, and Jim took their licks, laid their bunts down, and ran them out. Then Jerry walked up to the plate. He, too, was nervous, but he hit the first pitch solidly and the connection gave him confidence. He sent a hard grounder through short, passed up a ball, and then pulled a long, high fly far over Bob Green's head in left field.

"A homer in any park," Rip called from first base. "You really clobbered that one, Jerry."

That did it. Jerry smiled for the first time. Then he laid down a bunt and ran it out. Chip watched to see if Jerry would sprint all the way to first and nodded with satisfaction when the north-sider sped across the bag at full speed. Chip was walking up to the plate for his licks when Jerry came trotting back. "That's the way to belt them, Jerry," he called.

As practice continued, Chip watched Jerry and Turk closely. They both fielded well, and it seemed sure they could strengthen the club. Turk had made himself at home at once, but it took Jerry a little longer to loosen up. Later, Chip called off practice and excused everyone except the pitchers. The players took off for home. Chip noted that Billy Jo walked away with Jerry and Turk. *That's a good sign,* he thought happily.

Chip and Soapy worked with Rick Baracat, Franco Bender, and Michael until dark. Of the three pitchers,

Michael was the most promising. The boy had unusual throwing power and good wrist action. When it was too dark for Soapy to see the ball, Chip called practice off. Soapy and Chip walked along with Michael to the river road. Before they parted, the younger boy promised to be there for practice on Friday; Soapy and Chip continued on home, talking about the day's developments.

"I'll have something good to report to the board for a change," Chip said, pleased at the thought.

"This practice was only a start," Soapy warned. "The Colts may accept Jerry and Turk, but it'll be different with the rest of the high school kids."

"Rip and Billy Jo will take care of them. If I can only get to Mike Hogan. Then everything will be set."

CHAPTER 14

Hungry
Hurler

PETEY JACKSON was driving, Soapy was in the front passenger seat, and Chip had the backseat all to himself. The road to Camp Curtis was jammed with cars. Chip's only thoughts were of the upcoming game. Brighton and Curtis were both undefeated and tied for the Valley League championship. Before the afternoon was over, one of the teams would be no better off than the Colts.

Soapy was talking to Petey and his voice broke through Chip's thoughts. "Turk and Jerry made the difference. You should have seen them yesterday against Bradford."

"Everybody beats Bradford. Clarksville is tough though."

"But we'll take 'em. We'll take Brighton and Curtis too. Then it will be the Colts against one of them for the championship."

"Not with the kind of pitchers you've got," Petey said scornfully.

Soapy hooked a thumb over his shoulder. "You counting Chip?"

"Of course I'm not. He's got other problems."

Only one problem, Chip was thinking. Only Mike Hogan. Everything else was falling into place. The small-fry program was a big success, the high school kids were coming around, and the north-siders had completely reversed themselves and were solidly behind the fairgrounds project. If he could only find a way to change the tunnel superintendent's feelings toward Valley Falls, it would be a grand slam.

When they reached Camp Curtis, Petey found a parking place near the entrance. The three friends walked up the hill until they reached the ball field. The diamond was laid out beautifully with a small grandstand behind the plate and bleachers extending out along each baseline toward first and third bases. All the bleacher seats were already taken. The Camp Curtis campers jammed one set of bleachers, and visitors from other camps filled the other set. The grandstand had been reserved for adults.

Both teams had finished their warm-ups, and the game was just about to start. The three Valley Falls friends found seats in the grandstand just as the Curtis players ran out on the field.

Lefty Slavin made a big show of removing his warm-up jacket and took his time getting to the mound. The young campers went wild as he swaggered out of the dugout. The southpaw was in rare form and had evidently been given a lot of rest in preparation for this important game. He struck out the Brighton lead-off batter, but Speed Morris, batting second, got hold of one of Slavin's curves and drove a hard grounder between first and second. The ball nearly got through; but the second baseman made a good stop and the throw beat Speed by a step. Looking as composed as ever, Biggie was in the on-deck circle when the third batter went down swinging.

Chip knew his pals' batting strengths and weaknesses by heart, so he concentrated mentally on the other Brighton players. When Curtis came to bat, however, he began to talk to Soapy about the batters. Neither team could score in the first seven innings. Slavin held the Brighton batters in the palm of his hand. The Brighton pitcher had perfect control, and although he had been tagged for six hits, his teammates' brilliant support fully countered the blows.

The Brighton leadoff hitter struck out in the top of the eighth, but Speed singled and reached first base. The number-three hitter fouled out, and Speed was still perched on first base when Biggie came to bat. Biggie looked at a curve for ball one and then caught one of Slavin's fastballs right on the nose. The ball carried to the right-field fence and, although the fielder played it beautifully and made a good peg, Speed was in ahead of the throw for the first score of the game. The next hitter flied out; Brighton was ahead 1-0.

But Brighton's lead didn't last out the inning. The Curtis players finally got to the Brighton pitcher. Two hits, a walk, and a sacrifice fly resulted in two runs. The 2-1 score held up through the top of the ninth, and the game ended with Camp Curtis still undefeated as the undisputed leaders of the Valley League.

The return trip to Valley Falls was a lot faster and quieter than the previous drive. Chip knew Soapy and Petey had been pulling just as hard for Brighton as he had. The defeat had sent Brighton to the losers' division. If the Colts got past Clarksville and his pals' team also won their next game, the Colts's game with Brighton would eliminate one of them from the race. But Chip was quick to tell himself that games are won one at a time. That meant Clarksville was the team the Colts ought to be worrying about until at least next Saturday.

The Colts players didn't contribute much to the fairgrounds project the following week. They were fired up with baseball fever, and they practiced their hitting and fielding all day long, all week. The fever gripped Chip, too, and each evening when he was helping Bender, Baracat, and Michael, he sharpened up his own throwing as well.

Thursday night, on the way home, Soapy was unusually quiet.

"What are you so glum about?" Chip asked. "Are you worrying about something?"

"Well," Soapy said hesitantly, "I hate to say this, but you're losing your popularity with a lot of the high school kids. Most of them are saying the Colts could win the Valley League championship if you weren't afraid of your reputation. Others say you think you're too good to pitch for the Colts. To make it worse, Lefty Slavin has been talking about you at the Sugar Bowl."

"What has he been saying?"

"Well, Slavin has been bragging about beating you in the national championship game, and he's been saying some other things too."

"Like what?"

"Well, like you're afraid to pitch against him."

"But we haven't even *played* Curtis. We won't play them unless we win our next two games."

"That's the point. He's spreading the impression that you don't want to win because then you might *have* to pitch against Curtis."

"Even so, Soapy, I couldn't pitch *all* the games."

"Then you better do something about Michael. Right now, he's the best chucker you've got. All he needs is experience."

"All right, let's expose him to some experience."

"How?"

"Start him Saturday against Clarksville."

Soapy's head shot around, and he looked at Chip in astonishment. "But you said his father wouldn't let him play for a Valley Falls team."

"Not exactly. Michael implied that, but I've got a hunch he would give his right arm to have the chance."

"You mean his left arm."

"All right," Chip chuckled, "his left arm. We'll let Michael make the decision."

"He hasn't shown up for a game yet," Soapy reminded Chip.

"We never told him he would play in a game."

Soapy shook his head skeptically. "It's a pretty big step, starting a kid against a team like Clarksville."

"Not when he's hungry. Anyway, he's got to start sometime. Besides, I'm pressed for time."

"I don't get it."

"Do you remember what I told you about winning over the leaders? Well, Rip and Billy Jo are the high school leaders, and that was a big step. And, because of Speck Blaine, we're making progress with the north-siders. Now, what's the most important goal left?"

"Sure!" the redhead said eagerly. "Of course! Michael could be the Tunnel Town leader. Right?"

"In a manner of speaking, yes. He could help win his father, who *is* the leader. We'll start Michael Saturday."

"You think you can sell him on the idea?"

"I've got to sell it on him," Chip said grimly. "I'll talk to him tomorrow right after practice."

Friday evening, when he ended the workout, Chip asked Michael to remain and throw a little longer. "All right?" he asked.

Michael nodded eagerly. "Absolutely, Chip."

With Soapy catching, Chip helped the youngster until it was too dark to see the ball. Then he called a halt to the practice and walked along with Michael to the bench where the teen had left his jacket. "How does your arm feel?" he asked. "Tired?"

"No, Chip. It feels fine. You know, I feel like I could pitch a game right now!"

"Good. How about tomorrow afternoon? You think it will feel the same way?"

"I guess so. Sure!"

"Then you're starting the game tomorrow."

Michael's jaw slackened and he stopped short. "You mean you want me to pitch? Against Clarksville?"

"That's right."

"You must be kidding, Chip," Michael said incredulously.

"I'm serious."

"But that's a league game. The Colts *have* to win. If they lose, they can't win the championship."

"I know."

The boy shook his head in disbelief. "Chip, I've never pitched in a big game in my life. Besides—"

"You remember the first time we met, don't you? Over at Clarksville? That was more than a month ago. You've come a long way since then. Right?"

Michael nodded. "Yes," he said in a low voice, "I think so."

"Do you remember what you said when we talked that day? You said you just *had* to be a pitcher." Chip paused and then continued, stressing each word. "You also said that no one ever gave you a chance. Right?"

"Yes, Chip. But, still, Clarksville is a big team."

"That's right." Chip said quickly. "Now, let's think back a little more. You also mentioned Bob Feller. So, according to your way of thinking, Bob Feller should have turned down professional baseball because the teams were big-league. Is that what you're trying to say?"

"Yes, I mean, no—but Bob Feller was different. He was, well, older."

"A year older, maybe less. But that wasn't the big difference. He was hungry. He was a hungry hurler. Do you know what 'hungry' means in sports language?"

"I think so."

"I doubt it. Because, first, you don't know what it means to be a have-not, to want something so badly you can taste it. And until making good as a pitcher means so much to you that no sacrifice is too much, you're not hungry.

"Lots of players think that dreaming and hoping for things they want means they're hungry. Every athlete dreams and hopes he'll be a star. But the hungry athlete *does* something about his longed-for goal.

"*You've* been working hard for a long time to prove you can pitch. You've earned Soapy's confidence, and you've earned mine. You have a chance to prove yourself now. A chance to prove himself is all a hungry hurler needs. That brings us back to you. Are you hungry or not?"

Michael looked down at the ground for a long time. Chip could almost see the wheels turning in the boy's mind as he considered the words. Michael was undoubtedly measuring his own personal opportunity against the importance of the game to the Colts players. When he looked up, his chin was set and his voice was direct and determined. "If you think I should pitch tomorrow, Chip, I'll try."

"I hoped you would say that, Michael. Now get a good night's sleep. We're leaving in cars from the high school at twelve o'clock. Be on time."

HUNGRY HURLER

"Will it be all right if my sister drives me to Clarksville? She drives over there every Saturday."

"Sure thing. Game time is two o'clock. Be there by one o'clock so you can get in a good warm-up."

CHAPTER 15

The Greater Reward

CHIP'S HEART SANK as the Clarksville catcher caught one of Bender's lazy curveballs right on the nose. The hometown fans went wild as the ball cleared Rip Redding's desperate leap and landed in right field, a clean single.

The runner on second base broke for third as Jerry Blaine sprinted forward and fielded the ball on the first hop. Setting himself, Jerry threw a strike to Soapy, who was covering the plate.

It was a beautiful peg, and the lead runner, turning third and racing for the plate with the tying run, realized its accuracy and retreated to third base. The batter turned first and advanced to second on the throw.

The pressure was on! Chip yelled, "Time!" and started toward the mound. On the way, he glanced at the scoreboard. In the last of the ninth, with the Colts leading 7-6, a Clarksville runner was perched on third base, carrying the tying run. Another was standing on second with the winning run, and a pinch hitter was waiting in the on-deck circle. There was only one man away!

Rick Baracat had been the starting pitcher and lasted until the bottom of the seventh. Then, with the Colts leading 7-4, Clarksville loaded the bases. Chip had sent Bender in to put out the fire, but Clarksville had scored two quick runs to make the score 7-6 before the side was retired. Sensational defensive plays by the Colts had enabled Bender to last until now.

If only Michael had shown up . . . .

Chip came to the mound, and Soapy and Rip joined him. One look at Bender's face was enough. Franco was completely demoralized. It wasn't fair to subject the boy to this kind of torture. A tug at Chip's own heart reminded him what the loss of a vital game could mean to a pitcher.

"It's now or never," Soapy said anxiously.

"All right," Chip said. "We'll put the batter on and load the bases. OK?" Without waiting for an answer he continued quickly, "Give the umpire the substitution."

"What substitution?"

"Hilton for Bender."

Soapy pivoted and ran back to the plate, thumping his big mitt delightedly as he went. The umpire raised his arms and announced the change of pitchers, and pandemonium broke loose—boos and jeers from the Clarksville fans, gleeful yells and cheers from the Go-Go Kids. After he took his warm-up throws, Chip served four straight balls wide of the plate to walk the pinch hitter and load the bases.

It was up to the Colts. They needed a play at any base.

Clarksville's leadoff hitter was up. Soapy called for an outside curveball, and Chip snapped it in, knee high. The batter swung from his heels, connected, and sent a blur of white just to the left of Chip's glove hand.

His reaction was so fast he didn't even know he had gloved the ball until the impact spun him around. Then he saw the third-base runner stop short and start back toward the bag. The rest was pure instinct. He fired the ball to Jim Gray and watched for the base umpire's reaction to the double-up throw.

When he saw the base umpire hook his thumb over his shoulder, a spark of exultation shot through him. The game was over, and the Colts had won!

A second later, Soapy, Jerry, Turk, Rip, and Billy Jo surrounded Chip and hoisted him to their shoulders. The victory, the cheers, and the crowd's enthusiasm filled him with a great happiness. The joy and exultation were overshadowed by the even more important fact that Jerry and Turk had been second only to Soapy in reaching him and lifting him to their shoulders. They were truly a team.

The north-side kids were yelling as loudly and as happily as the Go-Go Kids. Chip had to blink to fight back the moisture collecting in his eyes. The reward greater than victory was seeing Valley Falls healing.

He was emotionally and physically worn out and was glad to get back to Valley Falls. Chip spent the evening reading and then went to bed. Before he went to sleep, he reviewed the game and thought about Michael. The boy's failure to show up could be attributed to four possibilities: he was sick or scared or his sister couldn't make the trip or his father had stopped him. *Well,* Chip told himself, *I'll wait until Monday, and if Michael doesn't show up then, I'll call him.*

Sunday morning after church, everyone was in the fellowship hall, drinking coffee and eating cookies. Soapy and Petey joined Chip to catch up.

"Soapy was telling me about the game," Petey said. "Congratulations. Oh, look, there's something I think you should know. Lenny Hawkins came into the Sugar Bowl last night with some of his friends, and I overheard him bragging about . . . about burning down the fairgrounds grandstand."

Chip smiled and shook his head. "You're kidding."

"No sir," Petey said firmly. "I know Lenny. He meant it. Just thought you ought to know. Well, I've got to go. I'll see you guys."

Mary Hilton walked up as Petey turned away, and Chip quickly gave Soapy a warning glance. He didn't want his mom to worry. "Take the Go-Go Kids over to the fairgrounds in the morning and let them help out," he said. "I've got to see someone. OK?"

The redhead nodded and rejoined his folks. Chip and his mother walked slowly home.

The next morning after breakfast Chip started downtown to look for Lenny Hawkins. Just as he reached Main Street, he saw the teenager park his sports car in front of Valley Bank and dash up the steps. Chip hurried toward the car and met Lenny as he came out of the building.

"Hello, Lenny," he said. "Been visiting your father?"

"No, I just needed to cash a check."

"Got time to run me over to the fairgrounds?" Chip asked.

"Sure," Lenny said. "Get in."

There was considerable traffic moving in both directions, but the boy wheeled the car around, cut across the double dividing line, and headed in the opposite direction. The timing and execution of the turn were perfect, but it was a traffic violation and Chip immediately grasped the dangerous possibilities.

"You're a pretty good driver," he said, glancing at Lenny. "That was well done, but you should have gotten a ticket."

"They have to catch me first," Lenny bragged. "Besides, the fine is only twenty-five bucks."

The car was approaching the north-side bridge now, and Lenny stepped on the gas. The posted speed on the bridge was thirty miles per hour, but Lenny had the speedometer at fifty and climbing. *He knows,* Chip told himself, *he knows there is more to this than the favor of a ride.*

When they reached the end of the bridge, Lenny turned right and took the river road. The road was rough, but the boy never slackened the speed. Racing along, dust followed the car like an angry swarm of bees. The sports car hit sixty miles an hour. Chip was glad when Lenny slowed down and turned off the river road to the parking area the gang had built behind the grandstand. The car slid to a stop while dust slowly caught up and settled around them.

"Here you are, Chip," Lenny said. "I didn't think you would remember me. I mean, you are older and all."

"I remember you as a nice kid," Chip said quietly. "Someone said you had changed, but I didn't believe it. Now I'm not so sure. You just committed two or three traffic violations, one right after the other, dangerous ones. But that isn't all of it. Someone told me you had been bragging about burning down the very building we're parked behind, the grandstand."

"I—"

Chip silenced him with a wave of his hand. "Never mind that just now. Wait until I finish. The traffic violations today were minor infractions of the law, misdemeanors. Setting fire to a building is a felony though. Do you know what a felony is, Lenny?"

Lenny shrugged. "I guess it's serious."

"You *guess?* You better *know* it's serious. Let's suppose you *did* set the grandstand on fire. That would be a felony. If you were caught and convicted, you could be sentenced to prison. You could never vote, hold public office, or secure a passport for a trip to another country. The conviction would remain on the records forever. And, far from least, your family would be disgraced and probably grieve about it as long as they lived."

Lenny nodded slowly. "I shouldn't have said that. I mean, I don't really want to." He sighed and looked away. "I won't, Chip; I promise."

Chip nodded in relief. "Thanks for the ride, Lenny. You have all kinds of potential, and I'm glad you want to do what's best for you, but also what's best for Valley Falls. Don't do something you'll live to regret."

He got out of the car, closed the door with a bang, and walked through the grandstand gate without looking back. Lenny did not drive away for several minutes. When Chip heard the car leave, it did so without the screeching of tires he had experienced with Lenny earlier.

Pausing in the grandstand, he surveyed the scene. Soapy had taken charge. Colt players, north-siders, and the Go-Go Kids were hard at work with picks, shovels, and wheelbarrows.

Just then, a small car pulled up behind the grandstand and parked. Chip watched curiously and saw a girl get out of the car, walk through the bleachers gate, and pause at the railing. He recognized her instantly as the girl who had been with Michael the night of his trouble with Jerry Blaine. He had a quick thought that the girl was Michael's sister and walked toward her. As he approached, the girl looked up and smiled in recognition.

"Can I help you?" Chip asked.

She nodded. "I think so. You're Chip Hilton, aren't you?" Without waiting for a reply, she said, "I'm Linda Hogan, Michael's sister."

"I thought you might be," Chip said.

"Michael said he wanted to turn in his uniform."

"I thought baseball was his big dream."

"It is—or was. He needs baseball badly. Our older brother Bill is a good athlete. He does everything well. Michael wants to be somebody on his own. I bet you guessed that."

Chip nodded. "Yes, I did. Everyone wants to be a somebody. Will you do me a favor?"

"Of course."

"Then take the uniform back and tell Michael I would like to talk to him. Tell him, too, that ballplayers always turn in their own uniforms."

"I will," she said, smiling happily. "And thanks so much for your interest in Michael. You're his hero."

The gang worked with inspiration during the next three days and, with the exception of the outfield, the ball diamond was shaping up beautifully. Thursday evening, after everyone had gone home, Chip walked up in the grandstand and surveyed the field.

The progress made was almost unbelievable. It was the same with the team. The players had spent long hours in practice and, except for the pitching, looked better every day.

He heard a car approaching and turned to look. It was a town police car with Chief Burrows driving and Mayor Brooks sitting beside him. Chip walked down to the parking space and met Mayor Brooks just as he was getting out of the car.

"If you're here for an inspection," he said, "we're ready."

"It's more than an inspection," Brooks said. "The town has been served with a temporary injunction closing the fairgrounds."

"An injunction! For what reason?"

"It's an involved situation," Brooks said, "and what I am going to tell you must be kept strictly confidential. Henry Hawkins requested the injunction. It is a legal court order, and we have no choice but to observe it."

"What about the game on Saturday?"

"You can't play it here. You can't practice here or work here as long as the injunction is in effect. I suggest you shift your practices and games to the high school field."

Utter frustration flared up in Chip. After all the work that had been put into the field, why would Henry Hawkins want to close the field? What possible reason could he hold to take such an action? What could he gain by the injunction? The fairgrounds hadn't been used for years.

CHAPTER 16

Afraid No More

SITTING IN the home team dugout of the high school field, Chip gazed morosely across the diamond. Dusk was gathering, sending long shadows across the field, and Soapy was locking the field gate. He watched the redhead wave good-bye to the departing Colts players, and frustration gripped his heart once more. His best pal hadn't been his real self since the championship game. Before that, Soapy had been the life of the party, laughing, joking, and kidding, bringing happiness to everyone lucky enough to know him.

Chip thought back to the day Soapy had quit his job at Brighton. He knew then, as he knew now, that the redhead had only one reason for quitting the construction job. Soapy wanted to help him with the recreation job and fight Valley Falls's problem. The Smith twins, Soapy's young cousins, had promoted the Colts Go-Go Club, but Chip knew the idea had originated with Soapy.

Thinking back to the Clarksville game, he remembered the delight flashing across Soapy's face when he
replaced Bender in the final inning. After the game
and until yesterday, the redhead had seemed almost
like his old self. He worked and laughed and had a
great time with the Go-Go Kids and the Colts players.
But the closing of the fairgrounds had knocked all the
joy out of Soapy. It had floored the Go-Go Kids, and, he
mused, Chip Hilton as well.

The injunction had caught him completely unpre-
pared, hitting him with the suddenness of an unexpected knockout punch. He had concentrated all of his
hopes and dreams on the fairgrounds project. But, he
reflected bitterly, Henry Hawkins, with one little
stroke of a pen, had destroyed weeks of work and possibly wrecked the one thing that had a chance of
pulling the warring Valley Falls factions together.

He thought back to yesterday afternoon when Mayor
Brooks announced the injunction. The mayor had
advised him to inform the Colts that the grand opening
had been postponed because of legal technicalities, but
that the game could be played at the high school field.
The players had been surprised, but they had accepted
the change with little comment. After all, it was their
home field, and they would need every advantage they
could get if they were going to beat Brighton.

Despite his efforts to stop the name of Hawkins
from entering his thoughts, Chip kept thinking about
Lenny. No wonder the boy had found it difficult to get
along with his father. The man was unreasonable and
vindictive. A blazing feeling of contempt and anger
swept through him. Then, suddenly convicted, he was
ashamed of his bitter thoughts. His spirit told him that
bad thinking was as reprehensible as bad deeds.

Soapy plopped down on the bench beside him and
broke into his thoughts. "Well," the redhead said,

"that's that! We're all set except for the pitching. You going to start?"

"No. I'm going to start Bender."

Soapy's lips tightened and he shook his head. "It's no good," he said grimly. "They'll kill him. Baracat too. Michael *might* have done it, but Franco or Rick? Forget it! You've been doin' a lot of throwing. I thought you might be planning a, well, a little surprise for Biggie and Speed and Red."

"The high school players deserve the chance to play, Soapy. It's their team."

"Of course it's their team. But they're not concerned about who plays or who doesn't play. They want to win the Valley League championship, and they think they can do it if you pitch. So do I."

"But Bender and Baracat are the regular pitchers."

"Are you kidding! Chip, get off it. They feel the same way. They're not looking for personal glory. They're thinking only of the team."

"I had no intention of playing ball this summer, Soapy. You know that. I was and still am tired of baseball."

"What about the Clarksville game?"

"I had no choice. There was no one left."

"Well," Soapy said ruefully, "you sure better be ready. I guess I'll go home. Coming?"

"Go ahead, Soapy. I'm going to do a little more thinking."

Soapy left and Chip remained in the dugout. He wanted to clear the disappointment out of his heart before he went home. Then he thought about Michael and it set him off again. He had been hoping the boy would show up.

Chip got up and walked slowly toward the main gate. He closed it behind him and snapped on the padlock. Then he turned toward home. Just before he reached the corner, a small car passed and slid to a stop beyond the streetlight. He glanced idly at the car, and then his heart leaped. Linda Hogan was at the wheel, and Michael was sitting beside her. The boy got out of the car and ran back to meet him. As he approached, Chip suddenly saw Michael's swollen lips and black eye.

"Hey!" he said, "What happened to you?"

"It's nothing," Michael said quickly. "I wanted to talk to you about the uniform."

"Sure. Go ahead."

"Well, I have it. It's in the car. I want to apologize for sending it back, instead of coming myself, and I want to explain about Clarksville."

"What about Clarksville?"

The words came more freely now. "I was, well, just afraid. I was *afraid* to pitch against Clarksville. Afraid I would lose the game. I'm, well, I'm a quitter."

"No, you're not, Michael. You might be afraid, but you're no quitter."

"I was afraid to pitch," Michael said slowly, "because if the Colts lost, it would have put them out of contention, and, well, there was another reason. I was mostly afraid I would lose the game for you."

"The only thing that's wrong with being afraid is that it can keep us from doing the right thing. William Faulkner wrote a short story called 'The Bear.' Did you ever read it?"

Michael shook his head.

"Well, in the story, the narrator makes the distinction between being scared and being afraid. The young hunter learns that being afraid is dangerous. Fear paralyzes us. But, *being scared* in some situations is a natural response—it can be good for us because it's what propels us to meet challenges.

"And, speaking of challenges, right now, you

and I are in the same boat. We've both got to prove ourselves."

"No!" Michael said quickly, "that's not right. You're different. You don't need to prove yourself. You've proved yourself lots of times."

Chip shook his head. "Oh, no, Michael. You never see the end of having to prove yourself. A fellow runs up against something new every day. There's always a problem he's got to face. Right now, you and I are facing a problem we've got to whip. You're afraid of hurting the Colts's chances, and I'm afraid of hurting one of the other teams' players. We're both afraid."

"That's not true!" Michael said sharply. "I know you're not afraid." The youngster hesitated and then continued fiercely, "No matter *what* Lefty Slavin says."

"What does he say?"

"Gee, Chip—"

"Go ahead."

"Well, he's been saying you quit in the championship game. He said they figured out the beanball thing and started crowding the plate, and you were afraid to throw anything close and walked a lot of batters. He said, well, he said you were yellow."

Chip turned away from the boy, fearful that the youngster would see the almost insane fury welling up in him. It was guilty rage, too, because it was partly true. He hadn't been yellow, but he *had* been afraid of hurting someone. And he had quit. He hadn't been scared—he'd been afraid. Doc had put it right. That's what helmets were for, and a real chucker *had* to move batters back.

Chip had control of himself now and turned back to face Michael. The boy's chin was nearly touching his chest. His shoulders were drooping, and his arms hung straight down at his sides. He was a picture of youthful despair, and the image struck straight at Chip's heart.

"So that's how you got the cut lip and the black eye," he said. "Someone said I was yellow and you tried to do something about it, and you took a licking, right?"

Michael did not look up, but he nodded his head. Chip was suddenly gripped with blazing rage. He had taken enough, and Michael had taken more than enough. Lefty Slavin was calling Chip Hilton a quitter in his own hometown, and a fellow had to do something about that, even if it meant a fight. Well, Chip was ready. More than ready!

If he had anything to do with it, Chip told himself, the Colts would be facing Curtis and Lefty Slavin in the championship series, and Chip Hilton would be pitching. He would start the game tomorrow and the next game and the next game, and he would throw any kind of a pitch Soapy wanted. And anyone who crowded the plate would move back or else.

While these determined thoughts were racing through his mind, Chip was conscious of a small, quiet voice still striving to be heard. It was asking if he could really pitch that way against Biggie and Speed and Red, but he refused to debate the matter. There were going to be no exceptions. He was going to pitch tomorrow as he had never pitched before in his entire life. He would *really* pitch! He would show Lefty Slavin and Coach Curtis and the Brighton players and Petey and Soapy and Rip and Billy Jo and the rest of the Colts and Doc Jones and Stu Gardner and, yes, his mother. But most of all, he would show Michael what it took to be an all-American pitcher.

With a sudden, almost angry move, he grasped the boy by the shoulder. "Look at me!" he said fiercely.

Michael looked up, surprised and startled. "Now!" Chip said. "Give me your hand."

The boy's eyes opened wide. Then, he slowly extended his hand.

"I—"

"Quiet!" Chip barked. "Make it a strong hand and give me a man's grip."

Michael's arm shot forward and they locked hands. "Now," Chip said, "as of this second, you and I are starting all over. You are going to pitch the next time you get a chance, and I am going to pitch against Brighton tomorrow if it kills me. And if I can't handle Brighton and I need help, you're going to be ready. Right?"

The boy's grasp on Chip's hand tightened, and his eyes flashed with wild delight. "Right," he managed. "Right, Chip, right!"

"Good! Now you go along home. Tomorrow, we—you and I—are going to team up to teach a lot of people a lesson. We're going to show them what a mistake it is to underestimate a fellow with determination. Are you with me?"

"Yes, Chip, *yes!*"

"All right. Now there's one more thing. When I was little, I learned a verse in Vacation Bible School that said, 'God is our refuge and strength, always ready to help in times of trouble.' We have to believe that and say we're never going to be afraid again. We have to say it and feel it and mean it. Can you do that?"

Michael nodded. "Yes," he said, "I can."

"All right, say it."

"I'll never be afraid again."

"Good. That goes for both of us, and we're never going to forget it. Now you take that uniform home. Put it on tomorrow and meet me here at one o'clock ready to finish anything I start. All right?"

The boy was off and running toward the car. "Right, Chip," he cried, over his shoulder. *"Right!"*

CHAPTER 17

Three Big Outs Away

CHIP TOOK a last practice swing and tossed the weighted stick back toward the batting rack. Then, kneeling in the on-deck circle, he glanced at the scoreboard. It was the last of the eighth, with two down. The score: Brighton 1, Colts 1.

The crowd noise was earsplitting. The piercing, high-pitched shrieks and yells of the Go-Go Kids would have been enough. But they had company, lots of company. Camp Curtis was there en masse—some three hundred boy and girl campers and their counselors. And they were rooting for the Colts!

Soapy was standing on the third-base side of the plate looking in his direction, but Chip made no attempt to yell. He merely raised a clenched fist and shook it toward the redhead. The Brighton pitcher was ready now and came in with an inside fastball that whistled across the corner knee-high for a called strike. The redhead watched two outside curveballs go by. The count was two-and-one.

The next pitch was a fastball and Soapy lashed out at it, driving the ball past third base and along the inside of the limed line, in fair territory. It was a solid hit in any league! Soapy raced around first base and sprinted toward the keystone sack. The left fielder sped after the ball, fielded it adeptly, and made the throw to the third baseman, holding Soapy at second.

Chip walked slowly to the first-base side of the batting box. Batting lefty against the righty pitcher, he could pull the ball away from third base, and a hit to right field might have a chance of bringing Soapy home for the run the Colts needed so badly.

The first pitch was in there, and he went for it. He connected squarely, pulling the ball over the first baseman's head. It was an exact duplicate of Soapy's double except for the direction of the hit.

Turning first base, he saw Soapy tear around third and head for home. The Brighton right fielder fielded the ball on the first bounce and poised for the throw to the plate. As soon as the ball was in the air, Chip took off, turning his head just in time to see Soapy hit the dirt, beat the throw, and score the tiebreaking run to put the Colts ahead, 2-1.

The stands were one continuous roar as the kids went wild. The pitcher had the ball now, and Chip breathed a sigh of relief. Taking a short lead off second, he got set to move on anything Turk Blaine put the wood to; Chip was ready to try for another run. But the peppery second baseman fouled off three pitches and then missed the last throw for the third out.

Michael came running out with Chip's glove and met him at the mound. "Only three to go," he shouted gleefully. "Then we'll take care of Curtis!" The boy's face sobered, and he came closer and thrust the glove in Chip's hand. "I'm not afraid anymore," he said quietly. Turning quickly, he ran back off the field.

Behind the mound, his glove dangling from his left
wrist, Chip polished the ball in his bare hands and
studied the scoreboard. They were in the top of the
ninth, with no one down, and the Colts were leading,
2-1.

As Michael had said, the Colts were only three outs
away from playing Curtis. *And,* Chip added grimly to
himself, *from Lefty Slavin.*

Before the game, he and Michael had been throwing, side by side, in front of the Colts bleachers. A little
farther back, Bender and Baracat had also been warming up. Then, just before the warning bell clanged, he
saw a man stand up and wave his arm in an attempt
to get his attention. Chip recognized Speck Blaine and
waved back. Speck smiled and pointed to his wrists
and held up his fingers in the V-for-victory sign to show
he was fine again. Chip nodded and waved in understanding before hustling back to the dugout to join the
Colts huddle.

Now a little smile crossed his lips as he thought of
the team's reaction when he had handed the batting
order slip to Rip and Billy Jo. He had listed himself in
the ninth spot as the starting pitcher, and when Rip
read aloud the names and came to "Hilton," the Colts
had exploded with a cheer that rivaled one of the Go-
Go Kids' better efforts.

The umpire had announced the battery, "Hilton and
Smith," and as Chip walked out to the mound, a bedlam of cheers and yells followed him. The send-off had
given him a tremendous morale boost, and physically
he had never felt better. His fastball was right on target, and his curves were darting as if he had the ball
tied to the end of a string.

Mixing curves and fastballs, he had been in control
all the way, holding Brighton to three hits and one run
during the eight innings. So far, none of the Brighton

batters had crowded the plate, and Soapy seemed to have forgotten the screwball and the slider.

The big end of the Brighton batting order was coming to bat, and Chip reviewed the batters he would face. The leadoff man had a good eye and had walked once, fouled out once, and struck out once. Speed was batting second. The fleet shortstop was a great push-along hitter. *No one, but no one, strikes Speed Morris out, including me,* he warned himself.

The third batter was Brighton's center fielder. He was a solid clouter. So far, he had walked once and flied out twice on long blasts that had sent Billy Jo clear to the fence.

But it was Biggie who gave him the most concern. Biggie was an eagle-eyed slugger almost as difficult to get out as Speed. But Biggie was far more dangerous. A flick of his powerful wrists was all he needed to drive the ball over the fence. It was Biggie who had caught one of his fastballs on the nose and poled the ball over the fence for the four-bagger responsible for Brighton's lone run. Luckily, there had been no one aboard.

Chip felt himself tiring, but Michael's words gave him the lift he needed. He put all he had into his pitches, and his effort required only four throws to set the leadoff hitter down: a fastball for a called strike, a wide, outside curve for a ball, another fastball that the batter fouled back out of play, and a darting hook that cut under the batter's wrists for strike three.

One away!

Soapy whipped the ball to Rip and directed a verbal barrage of taunts and challenges toward Speed. But Speed knew all of Soapy's tricks and wasn't going to be trapped that way. He was all business and not in the mood to exchange any good-natured insults with his fun-loving pal.

Right then, Chip sensed Speed's intent.

Soapy squatted and gave the sign for an inside fast-ball, and Chip set himself, took his stretch, and fired the ball at Soapy's glove, a chest-high target.

Then, a split second after he released the ball and before Speed flashed his posed bat around for the drag bunt, Chip dashed forward. Speed tapped the ball and was away, sprinting for first base. The speedy shortstop outran the slow-rolling ball just as Chip swooped down on it. Chip picked up the ball and sent a lightning-fast peg over Speed's head. It was a high throw, made purposefully. Rip reached up and caught the ball a split second before Speed's foot hit the bag.

Two away!

Chip felt completely drained. Every pitch was taking a big effort now, and he berated himself for his lack of foresight. He should have known weeks ago that he would end up pitching for the Colts. He was running out of steam. He realized he was far from ready for a full-game stint on the mound.

The number-three batter walked up to the plate, and Biggie replaced him in the on-deck circle. Soapy called for a knee-high curve. Chip served it up, a flash of fear shooting through his veins as he released the ball.

The batter took a full cut, and the meat part of his bat met the ball with a sharp crack. The ball took off high over Turk Blaine's head and winged its way toward the fence. His heart sinking clear to his spikes, Chip pivoted around and tried to measure the flight of the ball with Billy Jo's progress.

Running at full speed, Billy Jo made a desperate leap, his glove hand reaching high in the air. But the ball hit the barrier inches above his glove just as he smashed into the fence. The great athlete slid to the ground. Jerry Blaine, racing over from right field, picked up the ball and made the throw to the plate.

Turk cut off the peg and relayed the ball to third base, but it was too late. The runner beat the throw, and Chip immediately called time. He started out toward center field, but Billy Jo was on his feet now and waved him back, indicating he was all right.

The roar of the crowd had reached a crescendo on the play. Now it lessened to a hush of expectancy. Chip's heart felt too heavy to have gotten back where it belonged without help, and he took several deep breaths in an effort to relieve the empty feeling in his stomach and the pressure in his chest.

The tying run was on third base, Biggie was up, and Red Schwartz was in the on-deck circle. Soapy and Rip joined Chip in front of the mound.

Soapy was thumping the ball in his glove, and his blue eyes were full of concern. "How about putting him on?" he said.

"Red is a clutch hitter," Chip reminded him. "Besides, Biggie represents the winning run. I don't want to give him an intentional pass."

"Pitch to him!" Rip said quickly. "You got him twice before."

"All right," Chip said decisively. "Here we go."

"Play ball!" the umpire shouted.

Soapy went back to his position, and Rip trotted over to first base and got set. Biggie tapped his spikes with the bat and stepped into the lefty hitter's box. Biggie passed up the first pitch, an inside curve that cut the corner for a strike, and Chip relaxed a bit. It was good to get out in front of a hitter like Biggie.

He wasted one, a fastball low and away from Biggie's long bat, but his next two throws, sharp breaking hooks, cut too close to Biggie's wrists and brought the count to three-and-one. Now, for the first time in the game, Soapy called for the screwball.

Reaching far back, almost to the limit, Chip put everything he had into the throw.

He heard the crack of the bat, but the flight of the ball was too fast for his eyes. The third-base runner dashed for the plate, and Biggie headed for first base. Chip pivoted around and searched the sky for the ball. He saw Jerry sprinting toward the extreme right corner of the field and then located the ball dipping down toward the baseline flag.

Holding his breath, Chip saw Jerry make a headlong dive, glove hand outstretched, reaching desperately for the ball. Then glove and ball met, and Chip's heart skipped a beat as he waited to see the result. Jerry slid along the ground, his arm stretched far ahead of his body, glove facing up and barely skimming the ground.

The base umpire was covering the play and paused a moment. Then he jerked his right hand, thumb extended, high in the air above his head.

Jerry, tumbling over and over, still holding his glove above the ground, scrambled to his feet, clutching the ball in his glove. Then he ran in toward the dugout. The north-sider had caught the ball inches above the ground. It was a miraculous one-hand catch that saved the win.

Chip saw his teammates dash toward the right fielder and hoist him to their shoulders. Then, before he could join them, the Go-Go Kids charged out to the mound and managed to get him up off the ground. Clawing desperately to keep his balance, slipping from one side to the other and bobbing up and down, he braced his hands on a pair of heads with bright red hair and strained his body around in time to see a big zero slide into place in the Brighton ninth-inning frame. As the Go-Go Kids started a victory parade around the diamond, he twisted his head until he could see the final score slide into place on the board: Colts 2, Brighton 1.

The Colts had made the play-off series!

Then, for the first time, Chip heard the chant of the Go-Go Kids. "Bring on Curtis! Bring on Curtis! Bring on Curtis!"

CHAPTER 18

The Whole Story

CHIP WAS READING in the family room when the doorbell rang, and he heard Soapy's voice yell, "Anybody home?" Without pausing at the door, the redhead cuddled Hoops in his arms and headed swiftly down the hall, passing the formal living room and dining room and walking into the family room at the rear of the house. Rip Redding and Billy Jo King were right behind him.

"Did you hear the news?" Soapy demanded, dropping Hoops down on a wing chair.

"What news?"

"Then you *didn't* hear! Well, you won't believe it! Bradford beat Curtis this afternoon."

"No!"

"It's true!" Rip exclaimed. "Bradford beat them 4-3 at Bradford. The Curtis team stopped at the Sugar Bowl on the way back to camp."

"You know what that means?" Soapy demanded.

"No."

"It means there's no series. There's only one game to play. Next Saturday. On *our* field! Is that a break or is that a break? They have to play us at the high school field. It's our home game."

"Who pitched for Curtis?"

"Not Slavin," Soapy announced. "They're saving him for us. Or that's what he was saying tonight."

"You mean bragging," Billy Jo said.

"That's right," Soapy said. "Slavin said he wanted the Colts to win against Brighton so he could beat you again if you weren't too afraid to pitch against him."

The anger bit through again, but Chip said nothing. Even in his dreams, Lefty Slavin couldn't possibly know how badly Chip Hilton wanted to pitch against Curtis. Five days of practice wouldn't give him enough time to really sharpen up, but he would be far ahead compared to yesterday.

His mother had been upstairs taking a nap, but the sound of the boys' voices brought her downstairs to join them. She immediately suggested having a snack and invited them to gather around the kitchen counter for sandwiches, chocolate cake, and milk. While they were eating, they replayed the exciting details of the Brighton game for her. Later, after his friends had departed, Chip kissed his mom good night and trudged wearily upstairs to his room. Hoops padded softly after him.

Chip undressed slowly. He was tired, but his thoughts kept him awake after he was in bed. He thought about Lenny Hawkins, the closing of the fairgrounds, the almost impossible victory over Brighton, and now the unexpected defeat of Curtis. It had all happened so quickly.

One thing was for sure. Beating Camp Curtis and working out some way to win over Mike Hogan were two tasks that *had* to be completed before he could esteem his program a success. Once those two items were accomplished, he would see what could be done about the fairgrounds. He began to think about Camp Curtis and Lefty Slavin and was still dreaming up ways to win the game when he fell asleep.

Monday's practice was one he would never forget! The Go-Go Kids remained after the recreation program ended to watch the workout and to figure out how they could drown out the Curtis campers. The players were full of pep, and the stands were full of support. The high school teenagers were there to cheer on their heroes; Speck Blaine was there to check up on Jerry and Turk and the rest of the north-siders; and Doc Jones, John Schroeder, Petey Jackson, and Coach Henry Rockwell, just in from University, were there to manifest their support.

Chip had his practice programs all set for the week. They would focus on pitching, running, and the bunt game. When practice began, he and Soapy worked with Michael, Franco, and Rick while Rip and Billy Jo conducted the fielding practices. Later, he gave Jerry Blaine a chance to show his ability as a catcher. When the younger batteries finished, he took his turn and worked out with Soapy. His arm felt sluggish, so he made no attempt to go all out, but merely loosened up.

Later, he called a strategy session and worked on the hit-and-run and the bunting game. He stressed the advance of runners, the safety squeeze, and the suicide squeeze. He worked everyone until dark and then sent the players home. Tuesday, Chip followed the same schedule. With the exception of his own condition, he wished the game could be played the next day. The players were ready, sharp, and at their peak, game-wise and mentally.

After dinner that evening, the phone rang, and Mary Hilton answered the call. After listening for a moment, she covered the mouthpiece and handed the phone to Chip. "It's Mayor Brooks for you. He sounds excited."

And he was excited! "Chip!" he said. "Good news! You've got the fairgrounds back. The injunction has been removed."

"Really!" Chip said, his heart leaping. "What happened?"

"Henry Hawkins called me tonight and said he was withdrawing the injunction. He was rather curt about it, but he said something about his son Lenny being interested in the program and that it was the only way he could keep peace in the family. What do you think about that?"

"I think it's great. What about the grand opening?"

"That's up to you. Go ahead if you think you can get ready in time."

"We can make it!" Chip said quickly. "I'll call everyone tonight, and we'll be on the job tomorrow morning, first thing."

"Good! Butler will want a story for Saturday's *Sentinel,* so he'll be anxious to get some pictures. What would be the best day and what time should he be there?"

"Thursday afternoon would be fine."

"I'll see that he's there."

Chip thanked the mayor and replaced the receiver. He stood there a moment, trying to figure it all out. Maybe his talk with Lenny had been worthwhile. Perhaps, he reflected, all the boy needed to straighten him out was someone to show they really cared about him. Whatever the reason, he was glad. The big thing now was to notify Soapy, Rip, Billy Jo, Taps, Rick, and Suzy and have them pass the word to the players and the kids. The injunction *could* have been all for the best. Now the first game to be played at Colts Field would be a Valley League championship game, and the Colts would be one of the finalists, possibly the champions. What a way to top off the grand opening and the dedication of the field! If only the Colts could win!

Chip put on the kettle for some hot chocolate and told his mom about the mayor's call. She was happy for him. They sat together at the counter and sipped their cocoa. She listened quietly while her son outlined his plans. When he went to bed, he could scarcely wait for morning and the opportunity to get started.

The fairgrounds swarmed with kids, workers, ballplayers, and fans for the next three days. And, Friday night, as Chip stood in the gathering darkness of the evening—and the fullness of time—he looked around at the results of everybody's work. He breathed a deep sigh of satisfaction and a prayer of thanksgiving. *This,* he told himself, *is a miracle.*

The Go-Go Kids had gone home two hours earlier, but the evidence of their efforts was all about him. Pennants, flags, sheets, and posters were everywhere. They had used red and white rope, Valley Falls colors, to cordon off sections in the bleachers for the Curtis campers and the Colts supporters. In the grandstand, they had a space reserved for the celebrities who would take part in the dedication exercises.

In the outfield, the headlights and the steady purr of the motor indicated that Michael was still operating the bulldozer. Soapy, with the gift of convincing, had charmed Red Schwartz's father and secured the loan of the bulldozer. Michael had immediately demonstrated his proficiency as an operator of the big machine. Michael's sister, Linda, had driven him home for dinner and then brought him right back an hour later. Chip couldn't help but wonder about Mike Hogan. Why hadn't the tunnel superintendent checked up on his boy's whereabouts tonight and all those other evenings when Michael had been practicing?

The lights of the bulldozer suddenly shot toward him. The big machine approached the infield. Chip knew that meant the outfield was finished. It was only a matter of waiting now, until tomorrow when the gates would be opened for the dedication exercises and the championship game.

By this time tomorrow, it would all be over. The celebrities would have been photographed for posterity by the editor of the *Sentinel,* and the Colts would be Valley League champions or be relegated to the runner-up spot. Butler was a fine sports photographer, and one good picture could be worth a thousand words, but Chip doubted that the front-page spread the editor had promised for Saturday's *Sentinel* could ever tell the whole story.

CHAPTER 19

Grand Opening

PANDEMONIUM REIGNED as the Colts players dashed out on the field. Chip pulled off his red and white warm-up jacket and proudly watched his players run out to their positions. Turk Blaine was at second base, the keystone bag, and would lead off in the batting order when the Colts came in for their licks. Keith Hill, shortstop, would bat in the push-along slot. Billy Jo King, in center field, would hit third. Rip Redding, playing first base, would be in the cleanup berth. Bob Green, in left field, would bat fifth. Jim Gray, guarding third base, the hot corner, would be up sixth. Jerry Blaine, right fielder, would bat seventh, and Soapy Smith, behind the plate, would hit eighth, the usual spot in the batting order for a receiver. Chip would bat last.

Pulling his glove out of his hip pocket, he started out toward the mound, cheered every step of the way by the Go-Go Kids and booed good-naturedly by the campers and the Camp Curtis bench jockeys. It was a perfect day for baseball with cool breezes blowing off the river and white, fleecy clouds perching in the blue sky—and so far, he reflected fiercely, it had been a perfect day in every other respect. He meant to see the day end that way too.

Mayor Brooks had delivered his speech praising Chip, the Go-Go Kids, the Colts players, the northsiders, and the high school teenagers who had helped build the field and renovate the fairgrounds. He also expressed the appreciation of the board and the citizens of Valley Falls to John Schroeder for the continued use of the fairgrounds. Lastly, he voiced everyone's hopes that Chip Hilton's dream of a recreation park would someday become a reality.

Then the mayor dedicated the field and unveiled the inscription the Go-Go Kids had painted on the front of the grandstand: Colts Field.

Brooks tossed out the first ball, and Soapy caught it and placed it on a cushion that one of the Smith twins carried. Then, escorted by his redhead twin, the boy with the cushion proudly carried the ball back to the grandstand and presented it to John Schroeder. After the game, members of both teams would sign the ball. The Go-Go Kids had planned the ceremony as carefully as a Broadway play.

With Hal Lee stationed behind the plate while Soapy put on his monkey suit, Chip took his warm-up throws. Then he stepped behind the mound and waited for Soapy. The redhead came tramping out, thumping his catcher's mitt, and the plate umpire turned toward the grandstand and raised his arms to gain silence so he could announce the battery. But it was impossible to still the crowd. He gave up in disgust, yelled, "Play ball!" at the top of his lungs, and waved the Curtis leadoff batter to the plate.

The campers' yells dominated until the umpire turned and raised his arms. This was the signal the

Go-Go Kids had been waiting for! Suddenly, strategically, they produced pans, sticks, cans filled with stones, horns, drums, whistles, and every noisemaker imaginable. The resulting hullabaloo completely and decisively overwhelmed the Curtis contingent.

Soapy pulled on his mask, squatted, and looked over the Curtis leadoff batter advancing to the batter's box. Chip waited expectantly, his heart thumping in his ears, the beat palpable in his jaw.

Would the batter crowd the plate? Or would Curtis wait for a critical moment in the game? Would they wait until there were men on base, runners in a position to score, before starting their beanball strategy?

It didn't matter. He had long ago made up his mind that his reaction would be the same. He would drive back every batter who purposefully crowded the plate, drive him back where he belonged, no matter what pitch he had to use.

With his glove dangling from his left wrist, Chip polished the ball with his fingers and waited for the batter to step into the box. But, delaying his move as long as possible, the leadoff hitter killed time until the umpire pointed impatiently to the plate and ordered him forward.

Then, batting righty, the batter stepped into the extreme front of the batter's box and extended his body and elbows over the plate. Chip's chest tightened, and he felt the strength drain out of his body.

This was the moment of truth. Curtis had thrown down the gauntlet before Chip Hilton could say "beanball."

He knew the weakness would vanish after the first pitch, but he couldn't force himself to move. A chill of fear drove through his heart as Soapy flashed the sign for a fastball.

Then, without realizing he had moved, Chip found himself toeing the rubber and aiming the ball at Soapy's target, shoulder-high, on the inside of the plate. At the same time, he was conscious that three words were running over and over through his mind: *never afraid again, never afraid again, never afraid again.*

He stepped forward and sidearmed the ball in with all his might. His follow-through turned him toward first base a bit, but he recovered quickly and crouched in front of the mound, ready for anything. The ball flashed in, from right to left, and the batter collapsed. There, lying on the ground, the leadoff hitter watched helplessly as the ball whizzed across the inside corner for a called strike.

That did it! Two more pitches, a curve and another fastball, were all he needed to retire the leadoff hitter. The push-along batter, hitting lefty, crowded the other side of the plate, the first-base side, but Soapy had the answer. The redhead called for a screwball and shifted his target to the right. Chip snapped his wrist at the moment of release, and the ball cut viciously in toward the left just as it reached the plate. The batter fell back and away just in time.

It was a ball, but the batter got the message. When he stepped back in the box, he planted his feet where they belonged. Now, completely in control, Chip needed only six more pitches to retire the side.

Lefty Slavin was in charge too. He duplicated Chip's effort, overwhelmed the Colts hitters with ease, and set them down one-two-three. Swaggering off the diamond, he smiled mockingly toward the Colts dugout. That was the pattern for the first four and a half innings. Chip was throwing hard and effectively and had the camp batters handcuffed. Slavin was keeping pace. The game developed into a tight, tense pitchers' battle. When the Colts were at bat and he wasn't on deck, Chip sat with Michael, Franco, and Rick and analyzed each batter's hitting style and weakness.

In the bottom of the fifth, with two down, Soapy worked Slavin for a walk, and Chip came to bat for the second time. The southpaw held Soapy close to the base. Batting righty against Slavin's lefty offerings, Chip watched three pitches go past, two balls and a strike. The next pitch was a change-up, a wide-breaking curve that drifted in toward him as big as a Halloween pumpkin. He pulled his bat through free and easy and met the ball with the meat of his bat. He knew, even as he started toward first base, that the ball was tagged, soaring for the fence and beyond. With two down and nothing to lose, Soapy had taken off with the crack of the bat.

Chip tore down the first base path as the ball soared higher and higher and carried far above and beyond the right-field fence. He slowed down then and made sure to tag all the bases. Soapy had loped home to register the first run of the game, and Chip followed to score the second.

The home run put the Colts out in front, 2-0, and the Go-Go Kids practically tore down the bleachers. Turk Blaine went down swinging to end the inning. Lefty Slavin hurled his glove angrily toward the Curtis dugout and stalked toward the bat rack.

CHAPTER 20

Crucible of Fire

LEFTY SLAVIN was up. He advanced to the plate, kicking the ground with his spikes. Obviously he was disgusted because of Chip's home run. Batting lefty, he tried to play cat and mouse with Chip by backing out of the box whenever Chip moved forward to throw.

Each time, Chip backed off the rubber and waited patiently. After the third time, the plate umpire ordered the angry chucker to stay in the box, and they exchanged heated words. Then, putting on a great show of annoyance, the southpaw moved forward and practically stood on the plate.

Soapy immediately called time and, turning to the umpire, pointed to the batting box line. The exasperated umpire was now really angry. He jerked off his mask and advanced toward Slavin until they were standing nose to nose. Both were shouting at the same time, and the crowd ate it up. Chip could tell from the umpire's gesture that he was threatening to call Slavin out.

Coach Curtis called time and trotted up to the plate. He put his hands on the pitcher's shoulders and spoke briefly to Slavin and the umpire. The official nodded and turned back to his position. Curtis patted Slavin on the back and walked swiftly to the dugout. The umpire put on his mask again, and Slavin moved back into the box, carefully planting the toes of his spikes so they barely touched the limed box line. Then he crouched forward until his head and shoulders were nearly over the plate.

Chip could see that Soapy was furious. The redhead was angrily thumping his glove and shifting his feet in disgust. Soapy squatted and gave the sign for a tight pitch, an inside fastball. It was what Chip wanted, and he fired it in, shoulder-high and right on target.

The ball headed straight for Slavin's head, and the southpaw fell back and away from the plate, sprawling on the ground. The ball caught the inside corner for a called strike. Slavin scrambled to his feet, brushed off his uniform, and glared incredulously at the umpire. The southpaw stood there for a long moment. Then, shaking his head, he stepped back into the box. This time, Chip noticed that the lefty's feet were farther away from the plate, and Slavin stood in a normal batting stance.

Soapy called for the screwball, and Chip started it in wide of the plate. Slavin waited too long and when he realized the ball would cut in and across the outside corner, it was too late.

Strike two!

Now, for the first time, the redhead called for a slider. Chip fired it at Slavin's elbows and the southpaw leaned back and away from the plate. But the ball shot to the right, and Slavin's hurried swing was far too late.

Strike three!

It was the second time Chip had struck out the arrogant, show-off chucker, and he smiled grimly in relief. The leadoff hitter came up for his third time at bat. Chip had struck him out twice and he got him again. That brought up the lefty push-along hitter, and Chip fed him an inside curve for ball one, a knee-high fastball for a called strike, and another curve. The ball broke in toward the batter's wrists, and he chopped at it and missed for strike two. Then Chip snapped in a slider, which cut down and out, and the batter missed it by a foot. Three away!

Even though Billy Jo led off with a double, the Colts couldn't score in the bottom of the sixth. Rip flied out to left center, Gray struck out, and Jerry Blaine grounded out.

The crowd noise had never let up. The Curtis fans got to their feet for the seventh-inning stretch, and the Go-Go Kids followed. The result was unbelievable bedlam. Stomping feet lent thundering support to the cheers and yells and shrieks.

Chip had felt strong all the way. Now suddenly he felt weak and tired, and as he walked out to the mound, he experienced an unsettling momentary fear. He struck out Curtis's number-three hitter, walked the cleanup batter, and fed the Curtis number-five batter a fastball that he hit right on the nose. The ball rebounded from the right-field fence and only a perfect peg to the plate by Jerry Blaine held the cleanup batter at third base. The hitter went on down to second on Jerry's throw.

Chip struck out the sixth batter for out number two and breathed a sigh of relief; the next Curtis hitter was weak with the stick. Letting up a bit on the first pitch, he tried a slow curve, and the batter went for it, managed to hit the ball, and sent a slow roller to short.

Gray came in on the dead run, but he fumbled the ball! The third-base runner scored, and the other Curtis base runners advanced to third and second before Gray recovered the ball. That meant a run in, runners on second and third, and only two down.

Chip studied the next batter, the Curtis catcher, a moment and then decided to call time. The catcher had driven the ball clear to the fences in his other times at bat. A solid hit now would certainly tie up the score and could put Curtis ahead. He couldn't risk it. The logical play was to load the bases, but he wanted to rest a bit and let his teammates make the decision.

"Time!" he called. He motioned to Soapy and Rip to join him at the mound.

Soapy arrived first. "Put him on," the redhead said decisively.

"Right," Rip agreed, joining them. "We'll have a play at any base. Besides, Slavin is up next, and you've got him eating out of your hand."

Rip walked back to first base, but Soapy remained behind. The redhead's blue eyes were probing for an answer as he studied Chip. "You all right?" he demanded.

Chip evaded a direct answer. "I'll finish the inning," he said.

Soapy shook his head worriedly and walked back to the plate. When the umpire called "Play ball," the redhead held his glove wide of the plate for the intentional walk throws. Chip threw four straight balls. The bases were now loaded.

Lefty Slavin made the most of the moment. He retreated from the on-deck circle to the bat rack and looked over several sticks. Then, selecting one, he pounded it on the ground to test its soundness before sauntering leisurely up to the plate. He went through an involved batting ritual, tapping his spikes with the bat, pulling up his pants, and jerking the bill of his batting helmet. Then, glaring at the umpire, he stepped into the batter's box.

Fired by his desire to even the score with the mouthy southpaw, Chip called on all of his reserve strength to set Slavin down. Each throw carried every ounce of his quickly dwindling power. He used a fast-ball for one called strike and a screwball for another. Then, putting everything he had left into the third pitch, he reached way back and drove his slider toward Slavin's extended elbows. The disgruntled lefty fell back and away, and the ball shot to the right and across the plate.

"Strike three!" the umpire bellowed, jerking a thumb over his shoulder.

Chip started for the dugout, physically spent but mentally alert to the situation. With the Colts leading by a single run and the tiredness and weakness drain-ing his strength away, he had to do something about the Colts pitching. He glanced at the scoreboard.

It was the bottom of the seventh: Colts 2, Curtis 1.

One run's not enough, he reflected. Not with an aroused Slavin bearing down. Then, while he was pon-dering what to do, everything came into focus. He had hoped and dreamed for a situation like this.

This was the time and place, the big chance to go for broke, to shoot for all the marbles, to overcome the last big obstacle and win over Mike Hogan. Michael's father represented the jobs that would lift Valley Falls clear out of the doldrums and solve most of the town's problems. As far as Chip could see, Mike Hogan would never be won over except through his son, Michael, and perhaps not even then.

Prudent foresight gripped him then and stopped him cold. He couldn't risk it. Not when a baseball championship was at stake, not when the hopes of

HUNGRY HURLER

Soapy and Rip and Billy Jo and the rest of the Colts and the Go-Go Kids and the citizens of an entire town would rest on the slender shoulders of an untried pitcher, a fifteen-year-old kid. Especially when the kid was an outsider, not even one of their own.

His thoughts turned to Michael. But what about the boy? The youngster had said he would never be afraid again. And, Chip reflected soberly, he had said the same thing. What about *that?* Had he been talking just to hear himself talk, or had he really meant it?

Yes! he told himself passionately. He had meant everything he had said. There was more at stake than a baseball championship. This was the big test, the crucible. *The crucible of fire.*

Quickening his pace, he walked swiftly to the dugout. "Jerry!" he cried. "Warm up Michael."

He turned and grasped Soapy's arm. "This is it," he said fiercely. "Now we go for broke."

"I know what you're thinking," Soapy said. "This is the big chance. Go to it! Take me out too! Slavin has me so mad I couldn't hit a grapefruit. Put Jerry behind the plate. He's a good receiver, and you can replace him in right field. That way if Michael gets into a jam, you can go back in the box. All right?" Without waiting for Chip's answer, Soapy motioned for Michael and Jerry to follow him and headed for the warm-up rubber.

Chip's thoughts were racing. Soapy was right. He was going through with it. "Come on, fellows," he cried. "Let's get some runs."

It was wishful thinking. Slavin, deadly serious for the first time, was concentrating on every pitch. He struck out Hill, forced Billy Jo to fly out, and got Rip on a hard grounder to his second baseman. It was the top of the eighth now. Jerry pulled on Soapy's monkey suit while the redhead took Michael's warm-up throws.

Chip waited beside the mound until Michael finished his warm-up pitches. Then he slapped the youngster on the back and left him standing in the middle of the diamond and all alone on the mound, the loneliest place in the world, and with more, much more, than a championship resting in his hands.

Trotting out to right field, Chip saw an SUV streak up to the main gate and slide, tires screeching, to a stop. Two bulky men scrambled out of the vehicle, slammed the doors, and walked resolutely through the gate and onto the field. Mike Hogan led the way, clutching a newspaper in his hand.

Chip knew why Mike Hogan was holding the newspaper. He had looked at the *Sentinel* himself the first thing that morning. True to his word, Butler had made the story a front-page feature that was illustrated by several photographs. The shots had been spread across the columns at the top of the page. The biggest one, located smack in the middle, had shown Michael Hogan on the bulldozer.

The men stopped and surveyed the scene, checking the crowd and the score. Then Mike Hogan saw Chip approaching his right-field position. The man glared at him for a moment and then started forward. His companion said something, and Mike Hogan, his mouth agape, stopped in his tracks and stared in utter disbelief at the mound.

Chip reached his position at that moment and turned toward the infield. Michael took Jerry's sign, nodded, and stepped forward to the pitcher's plate to make his first pitch of the game.

Things happened too fast for Chip to think about Mike Hogan or anything except the game. Michael made the pitch, and the batter swung at the ball, connected, and drove a sharp single over Rip's head. Chip came in fast, took the ball on the first hop, and pegged it in to Turk at second base, holding the runner at first. Michael was erratic and walked the push-along batter, putting men on first and second.

The third batter waited the young pitcher out, but when the count reached three-and-two, he went for the fat one and banged a grass cutter between shortstop and third. Hill went far to his right and made the stop, but he couldn't hold the ball. That loaded the bases. Rip called time and motioned for Chip and Billy Jo to join him. They trotted in side by side and joined Jerry, Rip, and Michael behind the mound.

As soon as Billy Jo and Chip reached the infield, Coach Curtis ran out of the Curtis dugout. "That's against the rules!" he yelled excitedly. "Outfielders aren't allowed to come in for a conference."

The umpire waved the coach back to the dugout. "League rule!" he shouted. "It doesn't apply to managers and captains."

Coach Curtis tried to argue, but the umpire was adamant and waved him back to the dugout. The diversion had given Michael a little more time, and Chip turned to the boy and smiled. "Tough spot," he said. "Breaks of the game. How do you feel?"

Michael swallowed hard. "All right, I guess," he said weakly.

"Of course you do. A hit, a walk, and an error could happen to any pitcher." Even as he spoke, Chip knew he was trying to convince himself that he should leave Michael on the mound. The bases were loaded with no one down. What to do? If Chip took the boy out now, Michael might never have another chance to find himself. No, he decided, he couldn't, and wouldn't, do it.

He put his arm around Michael's shoulder and smiled. "We're just killing time to give you a chance to get your breath," he said gently.

"Right!" Rip added quickly. "Don't worry about a thing. We'll be up on the grass, playing for the bunt. Just throw it in there."

Rip and Billy Jo trotted back to their positions, and Chip patted Michael on the back. "Scared?" he asked softly.

Michael nodded. "Yes, I am," he said, taking a deep breath. "But I'm not afraid," he added fiercely.

"That's all I wanted to know," Chip said, grinning. "Just throw the ball as if you were practicing."

He nodded to Jerry, and the north-sider turned and hustled back to the plate. The umpire called, "Play ball" as Chip trotted out to right field. In position, he waited breathlessly, nerves on edge, chest tight as a drum. The boy deserved a better break than this.

He saw the base runners extend their leads as Michael took his stretch. Then, when Michael blazed the ball into the plate, he saw the batter lift his bat and punch at the ball, making the try for a squeeze bunt. The batter made contact, but he undercut the ball and it popped up in the air in front of the plate.

Michael ran forward, but Chip knew he would never make the play. Then he saw Jerry. The catcher sprang forward like a cat and dove for the ball. Landing on his knees, he caught the ball in the air with his bare hand and, in one motion, snapped it to Gray on third base.

The ball beat the frantic base runner by a step. Standing stock still as if he were hypnotized, Chip saw Gray pivot and make a clothesline peg to second base just in time for Turk to catch the ball and stab his foot into the keystone sack a split second before the runner slid back into the bag.

For a brief second there was almost total silence. The play had been so swift, so unbelievable, so unexpected, that everyone in the ballpark was stunned.

HUNGRY HURLER

Then a shattering, earsplitting crescendo of sound broke from the bleachers behind the Colts dugout. Chip turned to watch as the Go-Go Kids went wild.

"Triple play!" they screamed. "Triple play!"

CHAPTER 21

His Homecoming, Complete

MICHAEL HOGAN was still standing in front of the plate when Chip reached him. The boy was watching the Colts infielders give Jerry the hero treatment. They were slapping the north-sider on the back and yelling like maniacs. Chip grabbed Michael by the arm and walked him to the dugout. The young pitcher didn't say a word, but his eyes were filled with tears of joy. Chip slapped him on the back and shoved him down in the dugout. Right then, Chip knew, Michael needed a little time to fight his way out of the fog.

The Colts were still talking excitedly about the play. The relief in their voices expressed his feelings too. But Chip wasn't about to let himself do any celebrating. Not with one more big inning to go. The Colts had to get some more runs. Now!

"Let's go!" Chip cried. "This game isn't over. Gray, you're up. Jerry, you're on deck. Soapy, take the first-base coaching box. Billy Jo, take third base."

Slavin was on fire. He was burning with rage and determination. The Colts could see it in every move he made. When he faced the Colt hitters, it was three up and three down. He struck Gray out with three straight throws. Jerry Blaine went down the same way. That left Green, and the left fielder popped up to the Curtis shortstop.

It was now the top of the ninth. The Colts were still leading, 2-1. The Curtis team came hustling in for its last big chance to tie up the score or go ahead. Three little outs were all that stood between the Colts and a sweet victory.

The Colts ran out to their positions, pepping it up, looking more and more like a topflight ball club with every passing inning.

Chip walked out to the mound with Michael and waited until he finished his warm-up throws. After the last one, Chip slapped the teen on the back and winked. "Only three to go, champ," he said, smiling his confidence. "Are you scared now?"

Michael shook his head. "Not a bit," he said firmly.

"Atta boy," Chip said happily. Turning, he ran out to his position in right field, leaving Michael Hogan all alone to face the biggest challenge a boy could ever meet on a baseball field.

The Curtis number-five batter, a long-ball hitter, stepped up to the plate. Green and Billy Jo were playing deep, and Chip followed suit, moving closer to the fence. Michael's first pitch, a fastball, was wide of the plate. The second was a change-up, a curveball the batter hit solidly, driving the ball on a long, low trajectory between Green and Billy Jo.

The ball rolled clear to the fence, but Green's perfect peg to third held the runner at second base. The tying run was perched on second.

Chip knew Michael was going through all the torment of an experienced pitcher, but for the first time. There was nothing he could do except add his voice to those of the Go-Go Kids and the Colts.

Trying to advance the base runner to third base, the sixth batter fouled off the first two pitches. Then he missed a sharp-breaking curve for Michael's first strikeout.

One away!

The seventh batter tried to hit behind the runner. He fouled off the first pitch but connected with the second, sending a slow dribbler to the left side of the mound. Chip was sure at that moment that his heart stopped beating, but Michael fielded the ball perfectly, faked a throw to second, which drove the runner back, and then whipped the ball to Rip for the out.

Two away!

That brought up the catcher. Chip went into action. He yelled for time and ran to the mound. Jerry and Rip joined him there. "Put him on, Jerry," he said decisively. "Let's—"

"Let's have another look at Mr. Slavin," Rip interrupted and completed Chip's idea.

He ran back to right field and waited while Michael threw four pitches wide of the plate for the intentional walk. The catcher threw his bat down in disgust and walked slowly to first base.

Coach Curtis came out of the dugout again. He called time and joined Slavin near the on-deck circle. Chip knew what the coach was talking about; he wanted to use a pinch hitter, to put in a righty batter to face Michael's lefty throws. But, evidently, Slavin didn't intend to buy the suggestion. The temperamental star put on another show, shook his head, and waved his arms angrily in the air. Coach Curtis gave up, and Slavin marched triumphantly to the plate.

This was Michael's moment of truth. Slavin might just get lucky. The wily lefty hadn't been able to buy a hit all day, but . . .

Michael's first pitch was a fastball that missed the inside corner. Ball one! The next pitch was a curve that headed for Slavin and then whirled down and away, missing the outside corner. Ball two!

Slavin backed away from the plate and looked out toward right field. Chip couldn't tell whether or not the southpaw was looking toward him, but he knew for sure that Slavin was hoping he could knock the ball over Chip Hilton's head, over the right-field fence for a game-winning four-bagger.

The angry Curtis hurler stepped into the batter's box at last, dug in, and pulled his bat through in a vicious practice swing. Jerry squatted behind the plate and gave the sign. Michael took his stretch, came to the required stop in front of his waist, checked the runners, and made the throw to the plate. Slavin stepped forward and swung his bat with all his might.

C-R-A-C-K!

Chip didn't see the flight of the ball. But he saw the runners take off and he saw Michael twist his body around and fling the ball toward first base. Chip saw Lefty Slavin hurl his bat toward the Curtis dugout, reach up and pull the batting helmet from his head, and throw it to the ground with all his strength.

Chip's glance shot toward the umpire. The official was the most dramatic figure on the field. Despite all the confusion, he stood motionless in classic posture; he held his face mask in his left hand, his right arm extended in the air, and his thumb hooked upward in baseball's traditional "out" sign. Chip waited no longer; he sprinted toward the mound.

Just as Chip reached the infield, Mike Hogan charged out on the diamond and lifted Michael, his son, high above his head. The proud father was yelling and cheering and smiling happily. The Go-Go Kids were right behind the tunnel superintendent. They had erupted from the stands. Chip stopped to watch them.

While he waited, he looked up at Michael. The boy was staring down at his glove, where the most precious ball in the world lay—the championship ball, a shining white symbol of victory!

The Go-Go Kids swarmed around Mike Hogan, pulled Michael from the burly man's arms, and transferred the hero to their own shoulders. Then, as Chip watched the victory parade form and basked in Michael's big moment of victory, he realized that he, too, had won. Once again, his work and prayers had ended in blessing. The breach was healed. His homecoming task was complete. Once again, young boys could grow up in the supportive community of Valley Falls, the Valley Falls that was his own.

Chip threw off his hat and cheered and shouted his support for the winning team, the champions, the Valley Falls Colts.

Afterword

NOTE: Dad's dream was that his Chip Hilton Sports series would provide an opportunity for fathers and sons to share in the magic of Chip Hilton and Valley Falls. His original books touched several generations; the updated versions are touching still others. His dream continues, as evident in this afterword from a father and a son, which also reflects one of the themes in this story.

Randall and Cynthia Bee Farley

THE CHIP HILTON SPORTS SERIES has helped me a lot. First, it helped me to give all I've got when I'm playing basketball, baseball, soccer, or whatever I'm doing, and to have good sportsmanship. The books also helped me to be strong in any troubles I might have. Chip and his friends did these things and have shown me a good example to follow.

Second, Chip always wanted to help others no matter what the cost was. In *Ten Seconds to Play!* (#12), Chip suffered a black eye, a cut lip, and more to get Philip Whittemore out of a jam. In *Fourth Down Showdown* (#13), Chip misses a few games because of curfew to help Isaiah and Mark Redding. In *Hardcourt Upset* (#15), Chip and his friends lose a lot of sleep helping clear Soapy Smith's name of a chain of gas station robberies.

Third, it has helped me to do something else in the summer besides watching TV or going to the pool. I have always enjoyed reading books, but I never liked them enough to re-read them annually every summer and each time enjoy them as much as the last. Thank you, Chip, Coach Bee, and Mr. and Mrs. Farley for giving me such a good example to follow.

Joshua Neuhart
Student—Brownsburg, Indiana

THE CHIP HILTON SPORT SERIES BOOKS, written by Coach Clair Bee, have been inspiring our family for more than thirty-five years. As a young boy in the 1960s, I discovered one of Coach Clair Bee's books in the school library in Belmont, Ohio. I was enthralled with the characters of Chip Hilton and his friends— Taps Browning, Speed Morris, Soapy Smith, and Biggie Cohen—and their coach, Henry "The Rock" Rockwell.

I remember reading that first book, entitled *Hoop Crazy*, over and over again. Chip and his friends were teammates on the Valley Falls High School basketball team. Being the defending state champion, the Valley

Falls Big Reds team was expected to successfully defend its state title and had started off the season by winning the first five games. Hopes were high; excitement in the town was mounting with each victory, and suddenly it happened. Everything started to go wrong. The team was losing. There was a stranger in town, who offered hope with a new style of shooting the basketball and playing the game. Would he be the savior for the Valley Falls team? Would Coach Rockwell lose his job? Would Chip discover what was causing the problem that was destroying the team? I wouldn't spoil the mystery for you. You'll have to get the book and find out for yourself.

As the coach of a fifth- and sixth-grade basketball team at Bethesda Christian School in Brownsburg, Indiana, and a father of three children, I wholeheartedly recommend the Chip Hilton Sports series books. Coach Clair Bee was a brilliant coach and innovator. He wrote stories that are realistic and exciting. He used his stories to teach the fundamentals, strategies, and history of basketball, football, and baseball. He taught me about the importance of practicing the fundamental skills, helping your teammates develop their potential, persevering in the face of obstacles, and taking a stand to do what is right in spite of peer pressure. I became a better player and person because of what I learned from Coach Clair Bee's stories.

It is thrilling to see my son Joshua and his friends reading and enjoying the Chip Hilton series. They play on their school soccer, basketball, and baseball teams. Like Chip and his buddies, Joshua and his friends— Travis Penner, Caleb Adkins, Josh Silver, Jake Haeffner, Doug McGinnis, Josh Black, J. D. Thomas, Scott Poytner, and Chris Phillips—have experienced the sorrows and joys of losing and winning championship games. More importantly, they are learning lessons from Chip Hilton about perseverance, hard work, dedication to excellence, and teamwork.

To Coach Bee's daughter and son-in-law, Cindy and Randy Farley, I thank you for updating and republishing the Chip Hilton books. Our family and countless others have been inspired and blessed by your dad's books.

John Neuhart
Coach, Pastor, and Dad

Your Score Card

I have read:	I expect to read:	
⎯⎯	⎯⎯	1. *Touchdown Pass:* The first story in the series introduces readers to William "Chip" Hilton and all his friends at Valley Falls High during an exciting football season.
⎯⎯	⎯⎯	2. *Championship Ball:* With a broken ankle and an unquenchable spirit, Chip wins the state basketball championship and an even greater victory over himself.
⎯⎯	⎯⎯	3. *Strike Three!:* In the hour of his team's greatest need, Chip Hilton takes to the mound and puts the Big Reds in line for all-state honors.
⎯⎯	⎯⎯	4. *Clutch Hitter!:* Chip's summer job at Mansfield Steel Company gives him a chance to play baseball on the famous Steelers team where he uses his head as well as his war club.
⎯⎯	⎯⎯	5. *A Pass and a Prayer:* Chip's last football season is a real challenge as conditions for the Big Reds deteriorate. Somehow he must keep them together for their coach.

YOUR SCORE CARD

I have   I expect
read: to read:

____   ____   12. **Ten Seconds to Play!:** When Chip
                    Hilton accepts a job as a counselor at Camp
                    All-America, the last thing he expects to run
                    into is a football problem. The appearance of
                    a junior receiver at State University causes
                    Coach Curly Ralston a surprise football
                    problem too.

____   ____   13. **Fourth Down Showdown:** Should
                    Chip and his fellow sophomore stars be sus-
                    pended from the State University football
                    team? Is there a good reason for their viola-
                    tion? Learn how Chip comes to better under-
                    stand the value of friendship.

____   ____   14. **Tournament Crisis:** Chip Hilton and
                    Jimmy Chung wage a fierce contest for a
                    starting assignment on State University's
                    varsity basketball team. Then adversity
                    strikes, forcing Jimmy to leave State. Can
                    Chip use his knowledge of Chinese culture
                    and filial piety to help the Chung family,
                    Jimmy, and the team?

____   ____   15. **Hardcourt Upset:** Mystery and hot
                    basketball action team up to make
                    Hardcourt Upset a must-read! Can Chip
                    help solve the rash of convenience store bur-
                    glaries that threatens the reputation of one
                    of the Hilton A. C.? Play along with Chip and
                    his teammates as they demonstrate valor on
                    and off the court and help their rivals earn
                    an NCAA bid.

I have   I expect
read: to read:

____   ____   16. ***Pay-Off Pitch:*** Can Chip Hilton and his sophomore friends, now on the varsity baseball team, duplicate their success from the previous year as State's great freshman team, the "Fence Busters"? When cliques endanger the team's success, rumors surface about a player violating NCAA rules—could it be Chip? How will Coach Rockwell get to the bottom of this crisis? *Pay-Off Pitch* becomes a heroic story of baseball and courage that Chip Hilton fans will long remember.

____   ____   17. ***No-Hitter:*** The State University baseball team's trip to South Korea and Japan on an NCAA goodwill sports tour is filled with excitement and adventure. East meets West as Chip Hilton and Tamio Saito, competing international athletes, form a friendship based on their desire to be outstanding pitchers. *No-Hitter* is loaded with baseball strategy and drama, and you will find Chip's adventures in colorful, fascinating Asia as riveting as he and his teammates did.

____   ____   18. ***Triple-Threat Trouble:*** It's the beginning of football season, and there's already trouble at Camp Sundown! Despite injuries and antagonism, Chip takes time to help a confused high school player make one of the biggest decisions of his life.

____   ____   19. ***Backcourt Ace:*** The State University basketball team has a real height problem, and the solution may lie in seven-footer Branch Phillips. But there are complications. Be sure to read how Chip Hilton and his friends combine ingenuity and selfless service to solve a family's and the team's problems.

YOUR SCORE CARD

I have   I expect
read: to read:

____   ____   20. ***Buzzer Basket:*** State University's basketball team, sparked by Chip Hilton, seems headed for another victorious season. Then, in rapid succession, a series of events threaten to obstruct State's great hopes. Chip Hilton faces some of his most serious challenges and tests of character in yet another book replete with friendship, personal courage, and Clair Bee's exciting basketball action.

____   ____   21. ***Comeback Cagers:*** Five fast-moving, hard-fought games leading up to and through the championship game will hold you spellbound. The climax of this action-packed story demonstrates the strength of faith and friendship and involves a startling basketball play! Coach Clair Bee fans will hold their breath in suspense as they read *Comeback Cagers.*

____   ____   22. ***Home Run Feud:*** When big, rough, bubble-gum-chewing first baseman and heavy hitter Ben Green decides to go all out as a slugger with disregard for strategy, the team turns against him. His morale deteriorates and championship hopes fly out the window. Chip also faces a pitching challenge unlike any before. Don't miss this exciting story about the importance of teamwork to the game—what State's captain, Chip Hilton, calls "inside" baseball.

____   ____   23. ***Hungry Hurler: The Homecoming.*** Chip receives an urgent, mysterious request to return to Valley Falls for the summer. Read how Chip helps solve a major problem threatening Valley Falls while overcoming his own pitching fears and encouraging a young hungry hurler, as well.

About the Author

CLAIR BEE, who coached football, baseball, and basketball at the collegiate level, is considered one of the greatest basketball coaches of all time—both collegiate and professional. His winning percentage, 82.6, ranks first overall among major college coaches, past or present. His name lives on forever in numerous halls of fame. The Coach Clair Bee and Chip Hilton awards are presented annually at the Basketball Hall of Fame, honoring NCAA Division 1 college coaches and players for their commitment to education, personal character, and service to others on and off the court. Coach Clair Bee is the author of the twenty-four-volume, best-selling Chip Hilton Sports series, which has influenced many sports and literary notables, including best-selling author John Grisham.

CHIP HILTON MAKES A COMEBACK!

The never-before-released *VOLUME 24* in the best-selling Chip Hilton series will be available soon!

Broadman & Holman Publishers has re-released the popular Chip Hilton Sports series that first began in 1948, and, over an ensuing twenty-year period, captivated the hearts and minds of young boys across the nation. The original 23-volume series sold more than 2 million copies and is credited by many for starting them on a lifelong love of sports. Sadly, the 24th volume was never released, and millions of fans were left wondering what became of their hero Chip Hilton, the sports-loving boy.

Now, the never-before-released 24th volume in the series, titled *Fiery Fullback*, will be released in Fall 2002! See www.chiphilton.com for more details.

START COLLECTING YOUR COMPLETE CHIP HILTON SERIES TODAY!